THRICE PUBLISHING NFP, a private corporation
registered in the state of Illinois, reaches outside
the mainstream to publish the work of selected writers
whose efforts, we feel, need to be seen.
It's flagship publication, **THRICE FICTION**, has
been a platform for presenting this work alongside
exceptional artwork since 2011. **THRICE ARTS** provides
design and editing services to writers at large.

THRICE FICTION

Volume 2 • Issue No. 1 • DECEMBER 2020
RW Spryszak, Editor
David Simmer II, Art Director

CONTENTS

Thrice Notes

I did not realize that putting out the call into our media connections in order to pull in articles for the subject of "Cultural Appropriation" would attract so much attention in one way but, at the same time, no attention in another.

Responses to the Submission Call on social media (which admittedly can be counted on to instigate a certain mix of disconnect and entertainment) attracted the usual suspects one sees on, say, any public Facebook or YouTube or Twitter post. In other words, mostly garbage. Some white people got triggered. Unpublished writers said they won't do their precious work for just a copy of the issue in payment. People who say they stand for free speech – when they think the state isn't monitoring them – made angry comments about censorship. And the call itself went largely ignored once the social media posturing began and the participants started arguing among themselves. I was even chastised for not realizing there was already a huge body of work on the issue and if I wanted to know about it I should just go look it up myself. And that was all I managed to collect at first. No submissions though. Silly me. What did I expect?

What I didn't expect is what seemed to be the general acceptance of cultural appropriation as something no more offensive than air. People who had a stake in the effects of Cultural Appropriation went silent. And I was as disappointed in the stupid responses of the privileged as much as I was disappointed by the lack of ardor among the writers the subject most concerns. I wasn't looking for the disjointed posers who argue their lives away in little bubbles of word limited bromides back and forth on social media. The same posting dance we've all seen a thousand times before. I asked serious questions. But all I learned, it seemed, was that Vikings wore corn rolls too so I should just go fuck myself.

This is the point at which we insert the usual *"what's become of our society"* moan. But I'm going to refrain because I'm already well beyond that. I'm beyond the point where anyone can insult, threaten, anger, confuse, confound, or get a rise out of me. Online or off. This is obviously not the case with a lot of people, if the evidence of the word salad carnage the submission call produced is good evidence.

I was at first willing to take an article on why Cultural Appropriation is a false or unimportant issue, if one was on offer. But I found that people (I won't call them writers) who may feel that way are largely unable to string ten sentences together on the subject that didn't include loaded language, clichés, and suppositions that we should all know better by now. And I came to understand the arguments against its charge are pointless. If not baseless. So I put that out of my mind early. And, still, I have no proof that this particular thesis has no merit. However, if you feel opposed to the sentiment, we do now have a letters section. And I encourage you to write a letter. I'll be more than happy to publish your name along with your particular nonsense.

But more disheartening than all of that was the stone silence from writers who could be seen to have been directly threatened or somehow affected by the phenomenon. I went to online communities, passed the word around friends, was promised friends would tell friends, I wrote directly to acquaintances in marginalized communities, and put out submission calls. Not once, but three times. I got nothing. Not one word. Not one person of color responded to our call. Is it not as big an issue as I thought? Is it a phantom subject? Is it something people call up when they've gotten a few rejects in a row and want to lash out at the dominant culture? What? What am I to think?

You tell me.

•

It never ceases to be impressed upon me that the same writers who bemoan the lack of payment from small literary magazines with limited, out-of-pocket budgets, are the same writers who won't buy a sample copy to check out if their work will even be a fit. At least most artists are more upfront with the fact that they're careerists who only dance for money.

•

Along the lines of our new format, as you can see, we are trying for something a little more sedate. Shall we say, in the more classic mode? Yeah, it doesn't matter. But I did not realize (also and therefore related to the first part up there) I would be chastised, argued with, and even "unfriended" because there was no open call for fiction or poetry for this issue. I was also not aware that these kinds of decisions don't belong to us – they belong to everybody else. Once again, what was I thinking?

But it's true. Outside of the work on Cultural Appropriation (which was announced in an open call) the work presented here by Ann Bogle, Eckhard Gerdes, and Amantine Broduer was sought after by us, from them specifically, for this issue.

As we move along in this, if we move along with this, we will continue this set up. We feature one of the writers. Use a lot of their stuff. Ask them a bunch of questions, and publish their picture. In other words, they are the Featured Writer. We will then publish one or two pieces by two other writers in the role of a supporting cast. Then an essay (non-fiction) and, hopefully, a letters section. That last part may be the hardest to get going, but I would suggest any letters written in be about subjects we are covering here in the new *Thrice*. Or kudos to the writers. Or criticisms of the masthead.

In future we intend to open calls for the two supporting positions. But the *Featured Author* will be of our choosing. That won't be a matter of who I know as much as it will be whose work we like. Even if they hate us. So unburden yourself from the idea that you have to be nice to us.

Why are we doing this?

Because the old *Thrice* wasn't able to send so much as a contributor's copy to the people whose work we used. Our funding came from a few small donations from friends and lovers of literature. But no grant we applied for ever came in for us. So to send everybody even something as small as 1 lonely copy would be strictly out of our pocket. And some issues had as many as 30 people.

I know there is a big argument about *"if you can't pay contributors you shouldn't be in business."* This is the viewpoint of a conservative libertarian and therefore need not be taken seriously. But, for us, we would have liked nothing more than to be able to send some kind of honorarium to the artists and writers who, after all, made the old *Thrice* so popular. Well, okay, it was popular because it was free too but shut up.

We are moving ahead with the idea that donations will remain slim, grants will be withheld from us, and we will not become millionaires whereby this may become a mere hobby. In fact this is more than a hobby for Dave and me.

So the deal is if we don't make it free and have fewer contributors, **then** we can afford to send at least one copy to our writers and artists. **This is why**. It isn't because we assume we're going to make a fortune doing this. It's because Dave and I both feel, and have always felt, that not sending our contributors something was a strike against us.

You had to balance, I suppose, the way we ran things in the old *Thrice*. If you wrote something we used you didn't get any kind of an honorarium. But you were one of the many people who got published for the first time, or were one of the half dozen people we were approached about by author's agents, or that piece you couldn't place in more uptight, stodgy journals found a home. And I think that was a good trade.

Plus I can be nasty and say there are plenty of journals that pay for work, Mr and Ms Complainer That You Aren't Getting Paid. So why try us if no one else has paid you a nickel for anything you've ever done? But I won't. Even if I just did.

In any case you see the format. The idea is to watch our page for open calls.

And one last thing. The reason we're not using Submittable any more has nothing to do with their service. It's a great service. Except even for non-profits like us (yes, we are a registered 501c3) it still costs money to use. Three figures a year. And the first figure isn't a "1." This was strictly out-of-pocket.

From here on submissions will come strictly through email. And our publishing schedule will be officially "irregular." Which simply means if you want to place something with us your best chance is to be part of our family and watch our web site. It isn't too hard to ask – especially if you've had six rejections in a row.

•

How many people actually read these things? Let's find out. We want to put together a free listing of independent bookstores in the back of this publication. Name, address, phone number, web address, if applicable. No strings. Send us your info, we'll put it on the list. Just drop the line to me at **bob@thricefiction.com** and stay in business till next issue. Sounds fair to me.

RW Spryszak

Ann Bogle

Credenza

Now the house is empty of romance except for a potted flowering plant from my mother for Valentine's Day. No man has set foot in my museum since I moved here. One man has set foot. The owner's brother to see about the gasket under the toilet. The Comcast installers, twice. The man and his son who sold me the corner desk and cupboards. The cupboards have a name I'll remember before I'm done. I'm showing that I forget sometimes and am not always right.

It was Abe Lincoln's 200th birthday, so that is how I'll remember it—the day, the time. The years I lived in Binghamton, I visited Irish bars in the evening, and I had many Irish friends, not from Ireland, but Americans whose ancestors were from Ireland. And one of them told me he could move to Ireland merely by proving his heritage, but he stayed in Binghamton after all. He bought a house with a turret where his son plays drums. Later I wrote five short stories about him and about our plan to move to Canada, something we never did nor visited, even though we threatened it when Irish bars were closing, and we pretended to be bored by cloudy Binghamton. He had his birthday February 12, and I'd talked to him earlier that day. He was worried about the bathroom renovation, and he asked me to give him some paint—cobalt blue with copper in it—but I laughed it off, as if, fat chance I'd send him paint. He was not enjoying his birthday in the least, which distressed me. Perhaps I'll send him a gift certificate for paint.

He and our Greek-American friend, Tomas, sat in the first row and smoked in the original Jerry Rothenberg course. I sat in the back row with Deb. She and I smoked when Tomas and Michael were done smoking and before Jerry smoked again. Other people smoked besides. We retained everything we learned. We learned more than usual for a seminar. My presentation was on Dada in Zürich, and while I talked, Michael drew my lips in his sketchpad, and this drawing became a monument to friendship that started then.

When I met the other Michael in Texas, I dubbed him Michael to remind me of my friend, but other people called him Mikey, and I might have realized early but didn't or wouldn't that I was not replicating my happy days but was creating a bomb that would last a lifetime and that would turn out to be no one's fault, just something—a timeframe—that happened and that contained its own happinesses.

I wanted to say a few times that you are Irish, but you had said that already, so I thought it might not add much to the conversation to repeat it. It might add too much. I might put myself in the position of iterating stories of Irish men. My friend, Maureen, writes about Irish women writers and other Irish people. I went to one of her talks in New York about the son of a businessman from Brooklyn named James Johnson Sweeney who became curator of MoMA.

The rest I told you, that I began to write male characters in fiction for the first time—I began to impersonate men movie stars in the mirror—I crossed over. I thought I would refuse to finish my novel about Texas and leave it as a short story, really leave it that way, without writing it in the first person, male point of view, but in the third person semi- omniscient point of view. A novel that spans thirty pages after all the cuts have been made, story with a complex chronological design that introduces a novel that doesn't exist. The woman in the short story is less interesting than the man. The reader might care very little about her because she is emotionally frozen, immobilized in her apartment by her inability to make a decision about wrongdoing about which she knows almost nothing. The other people in her world are more active and engaged. She is a poet who writes three poems and contracts to write little or nothing. Someone being funny might think it's a novella about writer's block rather than about a rock band named ISM-GISM.

Marie Ponsot told us in her talk about the writer's duty that "sex" had been referred to in her mother's past as "rendering the debt." What we call love or banging. I like your Pendleton sweater. I enjoyed your stories. There was such an opportunity to see each other in the evenings. If only I hadn't sworn off shaving—it was awkward sticking to it all weekend—I saw myself as beyond shaving when I swore it off. Let's cut this up and send it. You might think that's the end, but no.

There was a man, a Harley Davidson salesman I met in A.A., with whom I ate at Perkins many, many nights. I told him he seemed Irish to me, though his last name was German. The next time I saw him, he told me he'd asked his mother who said he was three-quarters Irish and one-quarter German. Why no mention of Irish blood in his family before then? My aesthetician, Kathy, went on a disappointing date with him—the motorcycle salesman we had picked out for her. He sells cars now that the bottom has fallen out. It was the car salesman she found so one-note. Then he got pissed off that she had told him that on the phone, and that is how I came to avoid going in for salon treatments—waxes, haircuts, color touch-ups, facials, manicures, pedicures—something I was given to before that.

Hors d'oeuvre

The summer is not a child's summer, not fast and grimy and bored. It is a married woman's summer. I have white-pink fingernails and a pair of good earrings and white pants. I am not going to work or living here. I am a house guest.

There is a boat house and a raft of skis. My husband, when I met him, was an avid tennis player. Now he directs Swedes in camera angles.

It is a fact of my life that I do not know exactly what he does during work hours. I imagine one shot over and over, and it suffices for all the other shots. Bim lifts the model's chin toward the ceiling fan. Behind her is a stand of palm trees, and behind them, a wash of sea paints. There must be more variety and drudgery than that, but I rarely think of it. We are two separate people.

Roger is up and laughing. He is wearing a light knit sweater and white slacks. He isn't handsome, but he is poised, so he seems handsome. Two bold V's in red and navy cut down from his shoulders to his zipper casing. His face is tanned and splintered near the eyes as if he were smiling. Little blond hairs pop up around his watchband. Roger de Souvenir, I call him, but it's really Desuvier.

Roger lives in the house without his wife and children. He doesn't seem divorced; he seems married at a respectful distance.

Karen calls down from a bedroom window. Karen is Roger's friend. They have been seeing each other for almost four months. Roger calls her Our Lady Accountant, and the appositive sticks, like spaghetti to hair. Karen put herself through college and graduate school and never made the mistake of marrying someone to keep track of herself.

Karen and I are becoming friends because Roger and Bim grew up together. If Karen and Roger were to break up, Karen would disappear like mist, and another woman with a different set of interests would replace her.

Roger's ex-wife, Dana, used to be my friend. I don't ever seem to miss her; she belongs to another era.

Dana called recently, when Bim and I were still in New York, packing for summer. She had misplaced a favorite sauce recipe, one that I had asked for at a dinner party. I found the recipe and read it slowly over the phone.

"That's the part I forgot," Dana said, and I could see her suddenly, at the end of the table, her suede gray pumps and rich green dress; it was that green dress from that year.

Karen tells me that she is afraid of libraries. She orders books by mail. What scares her about libraries are unshelved books, the ones you thumb through while you are waiting for the elevator, because you realize that there are too many books in the world and you are holding that particular book only because it is lost.

I notice that I drink more when Karen is talking. I resonate. Karen reminds me of Gertrude Odrun. Gertrude Odrun talked about paintings and pleasure and symphonies in a way I can remember but not reconstruct.

Bim is a friendly, good-natured fellow. He is awestruck by light and angles and the night sky. He believes in things. Bim believes in God and loyalty and sports. He was happy as a boy.

I was never happy for more than five minutes; I was always setting up conditions for happiness and breaking them. Karen agrees. She says her childhood was stale, or her childhood was long, and her memories are stale.

Roger is taking off his sweater and dropping his pants. His swimming trunks are underneath, white and opaque. Karen and I will stay behind, lie on the dock in our suits and sunscreen and sip vodka-lemons. Karen is reading Kierkegaard. I am reading Colette. It's too hot. The words belong indoors; outside they aren't real. Nothing registers but the perfect tapping of my fingernails and the rocking in the water after the boat passes. Bim is driving, and Roger is skiing. I lift my head in time to see them wave.

Big English

I hit the pole on Whited Avenue a year to the day. The radio was driving. The seatbelt snapped my sternum. The acts the shelf life. Later, the kindred, octogenarian doctor prescribed Topiramate, approved to combat P.T.S.D. My brother the pot smoker thinks the doctor is Big Pharma, but I think he is a swinging, bearded, whistling, singing shaman who studies chemical sequences. This one mimics coca stirred with stomach acid or chicken fried in grandma's kitchen without the nasty side effects, without the downs, the I.B.M.s and 666s, the big old Gregor Samsa, the taste of tire smoke, ash or tin, the cash solicitation, the guns and squad cars in the ward, the next-to-nothing boyfriend, all sickeningly handsome as he says it.

Un Americano

Ann and User Name are going to a coffee shop in a northern city. The weather is predicted to be 25 degrees. The cafe has exposed log walls. User Name's apartment is in the warehouse district. The coffee shop is near the creek. Ann will wear black boots, black jeans, and a gray cashmere sweater dress. She will not look "great." She will look even. Her hair will be in a knot from not brushing it after washing it. User Name will greet her by saying, "You're right. You are tall," and Ann will think of their middle-aged grief, though she feels twelve and thirty-nine. He will be tall. She'll say, "You're tall yourself! I so like tall!" And they'll dive for a table by the window when the elderly lawnmower repairman begins to clear it to leave. Americano, Ann will say, large, wondering if you pay in sex for that or if it goes on a tab or ledger adding up to gestures that add up to sex or money that adds up to the same thing as sex. He's tall. He's appetitive. He orders a Danish. He orders a latté. His eyes are wide then narrow and brown. Hers are gray then they look away, toward the back door where a delivery driver has walked in, carrying a tray. Nothing is going to happen today. User Name has a missing toe, but she will not know that until the third date. On the first date, she will like not knowing. The missing toe will mean, eventually, giving succor, not for the loss of it, a blade fell on it when he was eight, but for his hated father, his father who stayed up late and messed around in the kitchen making apple sauce and cherry wine.

In a Basket

1

Elizabeth is fifteen when she tells her mother she has "done something" in Spain and is pregnant. The boys call it "doing it" and fourth base and "all the way." Her mother calls it intercourse. Intercourse is what a man does with a woman when they are married to make her pregnant. Intercourse is what the man in Spain does to Elizabeth after driving her from the ruin of the cathedral to the cemetery. He is Carlos Ramirez. His teeth are very bad.

Carlos is an officer in the Spanish army. He has a wife and three children. He says a prayer for them in Spanish and teaches Elizabeth slang words for body parts. The English phrase he knows is: God is the Father.

Carlos Ramirez is the father is how she ends up saying it to her mother.

Losing her period could mean she is pregnant, but not six months later, not in December after no intercourse since June. That is what Mrs. Tory has to tell her. At the doctor's office Mrs. Tory says, "Elizabeth has been where she shouldn't have been in Spain."

The doctor says, "You learned this the hard way. Save your trips to cathedrals for the daytime."

The Spanish teacher, Mr. Swetnick, tells them to stay with the group and not to go off on their own. The group bores her, the tourist places. Elizabeth tells Mr. Swetnick that she has gone to church and met a Spanish family and eaten jalapeños with them. So he asks her about the Spanish way of life. What she thinks is that the sex has made her smell different and that every adult from then on will know and sit next to her.

She doesn't think about Carlos. She thinks of his teeth and the ruins and the Spanish landscape.

There is a possibility of not moving, of not having fingers.

2

Elizabeth's grandmother lives in a stucco apartment in a little town on a certain highway that seems only to lead to that town. The grandmother doesn't drive on the highway herself except to go with the old gentleman out to the country to buy apples. It takes twenty-five minutes to get there. Elizabeth believes that her grandmother has seen all the billboards and consented to them.

Every Friday, when Elizabeth is a certain age, she packs a little suitcase and waits in the driveway for her father or mother to take her to Grandma's. Grandma calls the suitcase Elizabeth's grip.

Elizabeth has the pink bedroom with the empty closet. There is a crib in the room for her babies. She doesn't always bring the babies, though. Either she plays that the babies are sleeping in the closet, or that she is a secretary, and the babies are home with their father. The father is a different one every time. She tries to have him be one father, but the faces change.

She keeps records and uses rubber stamps and bank pens to fill in numbers. The work keeps her busy, and the light in the room is pretty. Certain trees grow up near the windows, and the lace curtains move a certain way. The perfume smell of the curtains makes her happy. The bathroom has the same feeling.

At the old house, Elizabeth's crib is pushed against the maple bed frame. Elizabeth can climb in with Grandma if she wants to, or stay by herself if she wants to. The room is never quite dark, so she can tell it is Grandma lying next to her, even though in the almost dark, Grandma's nose is too big.

Grandma crosses her legs and puts Elizabeth on her foot and bounces her up and down. She sings a song in Swedish about a boy and a girl and some horses. It goes like: ria- ria runka, hesta-hesta blunka, vas ka-ai ria, integrated pia.

In the first week of September Grandma goes to buy apples in the country with the old gentleman. He drives very slowly, and they talk. They point at places from olden times. He is also a widower.

The car that hits them kills him instantly. Something causes him to take his eyes off the road, not to stop when he is supposed to. Grandma doesn't talk about it afterward. She has cuts on her legs and blue and yellow bruises.

Grandma goes to live with the Martin sisters in their house at the edge of town. There are four Martins living together and one Tory. Two of the sisters are actually sisters-in-law. Before being Martins or widows they were something else.

The room where they drink tea is bright and filled with flowers. Elizabeth is ten or eleven, but the women talk as if she were older.

The days of the amusement park are over. That land is being turned into apartments and restaurants.

3

Elizabeth is not yet sleeping. She makes the sheep jump over the pole like horses. She has been to the State Fair and seen a cattle auction. Those animals moved very slowly in a ring. Men and women watched them and threw their heads back and showed their teeth because of the manure. A man next to Elizabeth opened his wallet slowly like looking under a rock.

The light in the bathroom comes on and spreads to the doorway of Elizabeth's room. Love rushes in, and she calls out to him. He doesn't come in, but she can tell where he is in the bathroom because of the water and tile sounds and the direction of his voice.

"Go to sleep now, Elizabeth."

"I'm dreaming."

"It'll be better in the morning."

Her mother makes a soft noise and movement in the bedroom. Then the light goes out and her father creeps back to the bedroom, touching the wall.

4

Mothers are not born mothers. The father tells the child something incriminating about the mother, something that explains their lives as a tragedy. "Not I," the mother says.

The mother has a menu and a schedule. She takes Elizabeth to piano lessons and tells her about the school board meeting. At night she sleeps, her face pressed into her pillow.

In the laundry room behind the washer and dryer and shelves of canned vegetables, below the window well and its faint cell light: his hammers and drivers and saw blades, the particular mallet he produces to scare them, brandishes and brings down with a smack to his palm. He has tiny drawers for each kind of screw and nail and fastener.

The brother starts most of the fights and leaves in the middle. Sometimes he breaks something or threatens one of them. He is too old for this family, but how can they deny him? He is bigger than any of them, probably a killer.

Elizabeth goes to Sam's room to show him that she is not one of them. She brings records, something he will like. He is a stubborn buddha in his orange room with pipes and hookahs in it. He wants the parents for himself.

Girls lose their boy names and boys lose their girl names when they are born. Elizabeth wants the new baby to be Tiffany, but her mother says that name is trendy. The baby will be David or Sarah.

Sarah will break if she falls, so Elizabeth is careful when she changes the diapers. The counter in the bathroom is dark gray and light gray with swirls in it that remind her of Grandma's hair treatments.

The cat brings home souvenirs and growls at the backdoor with her mouth full to be let in. Her name is Florida. Elizabeth picked her out of all the others because she hid with her claws out under the couch. The father is an alley cat in Miami, Gray Man. This is funny and connected to the man next door to Grandma who polishes his car in the driveway and keeps the curtains tightly closed. He has a wife, but she doesn't come outside. He is thin and bent over, and his slacks sag.

On the true or false quiz of current affairs, Walter Cronkite is either the Voice of America or Father of the Country, a trick question. Her mother can answer all the questions, but not during the news. Her father is in traffic while Walter Cronkite is talking, and her father reads the paper only on weekends.

In the yard are trees and exact flowers, each with a seed packet and a set of requirements. Elizabeth plants marigolds and violets and strawberries. She fills a colander with beans.

5

God is the wish to be better. Later, God is more or less in focus, more or less deserted. Someone is laughing.

Sin to Elizabeth is a certainty like *breathe*. Mrs. Tory would never lie or try to hurt someone by stealing or killing or swearing, but sin (as Mrs. Blanchfield explains it the afternoon in her bedroom) is what Mrs. Tory is doing in keeping Elizabeth from God.

The Torys go to church. Elizabeth collects Unicef pennies. She hates the purple dress and the blue corduroy and plaid one. She screams when her mother forces her arms through the sleeves and her head through the neck. She'll sit in the closet, and they'll be late again.

Mrs. Blanchfield says that what Elizabeth knows is not enough. Church is not the purple dress or the Unicef pennies or the man talking.

The Blanchfields own jeeps and make additions to their home. Mr. Blanchfield had polio and sells chemical fertilizer. Marcella has a canopy bed. Marcella has had her period.

The cars, on Tuesday nights, fill three streets for the Bible study. At ten o'clock, the hundred people file out to their cars and drive away, and there are no cars, just grass and black curb.

Elizabeth stands barefoot in the grass near the honeysuckle and lilac. The mosquitoes are swarming. The headlights pass her. The weekly gathering at the Blanchfields is a spectacle. To her, the trees and stars are Time.

Marcella takes Elizabeth to Mrs. Blanchfield's bedroom to

repeat what Mrs. Blanchfield says. Mrs. Blanchfield holds Elizabeth's hands between hers and asks Jesus to come into Elizabeth's heart.

Jesus stays there for weeks, comes at night like a rabbit.

6

There is a terrible storm, and Elizabeth and Laura are told by their mothers to stay indoors. They go outdoors, where the air is strangely warm, and the sky is ominous. Elizabeth has never trusted a blue sky. This orange, dark sky, at almost midnight, sends them running for shelter to the warming house. The German shepherd is with them and jumps against the walls. Elizabeth and Laura light cigarettes. They are more alive at that moment than during any other thousand moments strung randomly together. It does not rain.

Laura starts up a candy store in the dilapidated shed behind her house and invites all the children to play at its bar. Candy a penny. Gum a dime. The children sit on tree stumps and light matches. The boys, alone and together, take opportunities. They call it the sex room, and Donald Dittmeyer reads aloud from the sex manual until he gets to public hair. No one can figure it out or stop laughing. This is like throwing eggs and tomatoes at the neighbor's house and taking the kindergarten boy to the rooftop and leaving him there. Elizabeth tugs the pants from the boy then throws her arms around him when he bursts out crying. Donald and the others say, "Let's go," and climb down, calling, *We've got your toy, little boy, it's all bottled up. We're going to sell it, and you won't have it to pee with. You'll never pee again.*

Donald and Jeremy chase Elizabeth over the grass between oak trees and around wide turns. Laura is with them and runs much faster than Elizabeth away, toward the baseball diamond, where they're supposed to be playing softball.

Elizabeth is not yet a child, something she has decided but not said.

She runs in slow motion toward the fifth-grade teachers, to their picnic table, hurls her body at the ground and grabs at watermelons, fifteen of them, to anchor her. She feels lost among boulders.

The boys take her by her arms and legs down the slope to the water. Mr. Easter is smirking with his head down, and Miss Woodchuck, not looking up from the melons, says, "Boys, stop flirting with the girls. Boys, stop flirting with the girls."

The grass is tall. They take turns peeling her, clothes, swimming suit. It is the same lake, same park, same thing her brother did in the water. Run not touching the bottom. Run against the water away from his fingers and toe.

When the picnic is over, and they are riding back to school on the bus, the others have found out about it. Someone asks Elizabeth exactly what happened. Elizabeth is not sure what to say about it. She thinks, Boys stop flirting, girls stop flirting, boys, girls. She was the only girl, though, so she is somehow responsible.

In the girls' lavatory before the final hour, Elizabeth is the center. There are not names for it yet, this famousness. The best she can do is point to what is missing, say, here, but not here, here in this place is an absence, a blank space that contains.

7

The underbelly of the bull fish is white and taut and full. Elizabeth tugs on the line, without winding, and swings the fish to the floor of the rowboat. The boat rocks. Her father has shown her how to wind her line and cast. He has also taken over for her. She is not only like her mother. Elizabeth watches as he takes the fish off the hook. She watches the desperate eyes. It doesn't concern her, her squeamishness about the gritty worms or her fear of fish fins. She can still go fishing and hate death. The father can take her out and belong to the day, the lake, the line of trees above the boathouse.

8

Julia sits across from Elizabeth in seventh grade math class, but not in social studies, where the teacher believes in free seating.

The social studies teacher tells the class about his first child, how beautiful his wife became when she was pregnant, and how perfect the child is and named after him, William the third. William plus three middle names and the last name, the man's name, Barth. He explains how he and his wife timed the conception to increase their chances of a son.

Mr. Barth tells about camping in Alaska, how large the fish were, and how dirty he and his friends became without showers. Brushing their teeth was the one thing they could do to feel clean all over. The teeth are the important thing.

Donald sits in the back of the class and makes a sexual gesture: a hole with his thumb curved, and pushes his finger in and out. He says, and the class is laughing, there are more important things than teeth.

Julia and Elizabeth become friends. Julia thinks that Elizabeth is probably her favorite person, not counting her family; families count but in a different way.

The boys who like Julia ask her to high school football games, as a way of acting older than they are. Julia is a good kisser and has big tits and a nice ass and great legs and a dark snatch—that is what Donald tells Jeremy. The four of them meet in the bunkhouse and make-out. In the dark, Donald and Julia in their bundle, and Jeremy and Elizabeth in theirs, Julia and Elizabeth talk. Julia says, "I feel like Barbie, and Ken here has kung-fu grip."

One day in the bunkhouse Julia and Elizabeth are cold. They get the short boy, Steve Market, to hold their extra hands. Steve is willing to be where sex is without getting sex.

One thing that Elizabeth has heard about boys, from her mother who knows this for a fact: Boys don't like smart girls. Julia must be dumb since her grades are bad. Elizabeth asks, "Are you dumb?" and Julia says, "I think I must be."

Julia and Elizabeth put their faces on and use curling irons. They have a certain laugh and a way of getting around babysitters. They say, under bushes and in the dark, their breath visible, that nothing the other could do could make a difference, the other is just right, a perfect person.

A popular girl tells Elizabeth that Julia is a slut. How can a virgin be a slut? she asks, but it is too late. Elizabeth tells Julia that they cannot be friends anymore. Julia cries, "Why do you care what people think?" They would have gone to Florida in August. Julia's parents took Elizabeth everywhere. She was a good influence.

Another popular girl writes letters to Elizabeth and delivers them while her mother waits in the driveway with the car running. The letters say that Elizabeth is special and deserving in God's eyes and that God has intended her to show her light to everyone.

Cassandra is very smart. Cassandra's mother can tell them about breastfeeding as it affected Cassandra's size. The mother's breasts were dry, so Cassandra got substitutes, goat milk, so her thighs are big. Their dog is a pug named Silly, and the father is silent and edgy. Cassandra's father wears a parka in winter and builds an ice slide for inner tubes.

Cassandra is too smart to be popular, but she has the cutest boyfriends, something no one can figure out.

9

Elizabeth loves Kyle, a neighbor boy. He plays with her body like the others, but with him, she likes it. She can't explain this difference between him and the others.

She watches from her bedroom window, until three in the morning, when Kyle comes home in the Corvette with his girlfriend. Kyle's girlfriends are always blond and with him long enough for there to be heartbreak.

For a while it seems that Kyle and Julia might get together, but Julia has brown hair.

The other boys, four or five of them, who jump Elizabeth in her own yard, and whose jaws and chests she kicks, have no girlfriends. Not even J.D., who talks with her about what matters to him, about mature things and feelings. He helps her pick out denim overalls. Then he and the others get her out of the overalls and kick sand on them behind the warming house.

They tell her that only girls kick. So it's weaker, disgusting. They punch and they attack the parts of her body that they lack. That's what? That's normal, not disgusting.

She retaliates until she knees J.D. in the groin, and he punches her in the pubic bone with all his force. Her leg is strong enough to cause pain, so there are sanctions against it.

10

Far enough beyond the last episodes of childhood for the life to belong to someone else, Elizabeth steps off the bus in Des Moines with a usable memory that spans four years. Sarah and her father are also at the wedding. Mrs. Tory flew to Atlanta to be a delegate in a convention for handicapped children. Her brother, now Samuel, lies sleeping near a boulder. Farm work, he mentioned in a postcard from over a year.

Kitty from the small town in Iowa, a branch of the family that barely touches Elizabeth's, marries Bob the Same One she has known since high school. It is a big thing, a holy procedure. Good of Elizabeth to take the bus all the way from Syracuse. Where exactly is Syracuse? Dad and Sarah drove down from Eau Claire.

Elizabeth mentions what clearly makes them edgy. She and Walter Lux live together. Next year, she may be standing at the altar, Kitty smiling behind her from the pew. Her father talks about virgins again: He was one and he married one. This giving away of daughters that he likes to be a part of, a regular wedding buff.

Kitty sits coyly with Elizabeth's father, knowing him no better than the mailman, and plucks at the folds of her gown. The dress is beautiful and belongs to her, to Kitty alone, after much deliberation and expense. It will hang for years in plastic sheaths in a spare closet until her children pull it down. What is this, Mother? What dress?

Elizabeth found her mother's dress in the back of her own closet. Crinoline or something and orangey-brown. Original—the newspaper called it—in beautiful shades of copper and pewter. It sounds like tarnish but is hand-sewn.

Her mother honors the forms. She lives among trees, plants,

flowers, hedges, knows Latin and common and regional variations. She administers to the specially abled: to prisoners and partners of divorce. Childhoods the mother won't discuss.

The father has ordinary memories. His mother was too protective. His father was too quiet. He had friends, a collection of physical deformities: eyes, ears, lungs, a dog named Spam, and in his living room, a whatnot shelf that caught his imagination.

Walter Lux is a large animal, a bear, most likely, who wants to reveal the senseless world, that part a coyote. Walter the coyote stretches all over the world without killing the weak ones he comes upon, a bear without fangs or claws. His anger is impotent because he is unwilling to kill. To kill another creature, to strike at it, or take its will is a Roman idea and Walter is more Chinese.

11

The world where she lives is a Roman world. Always something violent is necessary, something painful to feel alive, even at the moment of death, to feel involved, transgressed.

Thou shalt not commit adultery.

If the offender is a minor and is not married, and the victim is a minor and is not married, no crime has occurred. If the offender is an adult, there is plea-bargaining. Thirteen in Spain, sixteen if deceit is used and the parent complains.

Thou shalt not steal.

There is another voice, not the protagonist's. It is possible to forgive completely.

Each activity that honors life: washing, mail delivery, sunbathing, swimming, sleeping, rising, lovemaking, breakfast.

Arguing is her last resort. She argues with people who love her, and not with people whom she does not love. Certain people develop attachments to her that harm them. These people do not regard themselves first and still are capable of feeling pain.

Strangers cannot possibly love her, unless they are foolish. They confirm what she knows to be true of herself: Sex happens freely, without love and commitment, without the product being children, without sacrifice. That much must be protected: The body cannot be given or consumed. The body is destructible.

Habits die hard.

Good habits die easily. What is ultimately good may simply be harder to accomplish.

It is not true that she loves her face and body, as evidenced by so much vanity and attention to details of appearance. This is the work of a mortician, preparing the body for burial, disguising it for dealings in the outside world.

When she wakes she shows her ugliness and beauty. Strangers recognize her.

The girlfriends provide mixture and shelter. Elizabeth calls them my friends and within that designation are a hundred variations. One friend tells her that she has a gift for friendship. Walter Lux says, during the Newlywed Game, that Elizabeth is not as good at friendship as she imagines. Walter is not as good at cooking.

The friends' boyfriends make comments about bad housekeeping. Everyone wants the old order, but the old order is no longer possible.

12

Plot is a basket. *Forme is power.*

In another story, the story of many stories, girl leaves family for marriage, disappoints family by turning out not to be a breadwinning prostitute after all, finds love in arms and eyes of tall, guiltless thief, not a horse thief, but a wife thief, his weakness with women, his strength over men. Macheath, who is the criminal, and the father and mother, who are the brokers of crimes, give shape to the basket, and the daughter, who believes in love, is the handle of the basket, something related to the basket but not the basket, who does not hold or carry, but by which matter is held or contained or carried by the hand.

The prostitutes and wives are violets on the basket, jealous violets who hate one another.

In another version Macheath is incidental to the moods and

nerves of the women at any given time. The women share him between them like breaking bread.

It could be that the love partner in any given crime plot or story is the man as he views himself. The women, in the story of the man, are the brooms we all danced with in childhood and whose bristles we kissed and added buttons for eyes.

Viewable women, in other words, whose inner lives and moods remain invisible, the metaphor being their genitals, and the metaphor for men being men's genitals: his telescope.

The sheathed penis, the uncircumcised penis, creates another situation, one worth studying. That initial violence that balds him and makes him vulnerable, and then, invulnerable, certain shades of feeling lost due to constant exposure.

With the genitals as metaphor, the women remain hidden and the men go to look for themselves like hunting.

13

In cats sex is less important. Florida hunts. Ruby drools.

Elizabeth Tory meets Molly Devine on a visit to Northwestern.

Molly will not discuss her childhood but has let Elizabeth know that she loves her mother for her fortitude and hates her father for his alcoholism. Elizabeth blames her mother because her father hides and swaggers. For both women, someone is accountable.

Some people who know Molly want to be her. They imagine that she has money and that she is in full control of sorrow. They want to soak up her power for themselves. Molly's boyfriends teach her how to live peacefully with people who are inferior to her. Elizabeth learns from Molly that there is another way to be a woman. There is a way to play dirty and live.

Molly compares Elizabeth to Elizabeth's little cat, Ruby, who clamors at the door to be let outside then cowers in the whole world on the doorstep. Ruby is not like Florida. Florida bit and Florida hunted.

14

Molly Devine and Elizabeth Tory and Marcia Carpenter (another person who will remain hidden, no doubt) go dining. They order tossed salads and diet mustard and mineral water, which they have begun to drink in lieu of sugar pop, because of the calories, and to allow them to drink more thick, heavy Irish beer at a later sitting. Molly destroys her napkin with her fork while they wait for the food to come. Elizabeth thinks of things she cannot say, and Molly and Marcia, like two boys in their affinity to athletics, rib one another, without possibly actually touching, a sort of winking that goes on or a similarity in tone and joke to let Elizabeth know that she is the girl among them.

Elizabeth studies her own left hand. It is swollen and has a funny, sick color. She wears her grandmother's rings: a high school band from 1912 and another ring, a moonstone for turning eighteen. The grandmother was already teaching by then, driving a horse and buggy to a one-room schoolhouse where farm children gathered, six to twenty years in age.

Molly and Elizabeth and Marcia read their placemats: a game of golf that you play with pencil and closing your eyes until the tip of the pencil goes into a sand trap or into the woods or river. Molly is best at the game. She is coordinated and has the best inner eye.

Elizabeth thinks of Molly's father playing golf all day, and how he is at that moment drinking martinis, playing golf, while the three women are sitting three hundred miles away playing placemat golf, not drinking martinis.

Molly opens her eye to see where she has stopped the pencil. It is a hole in one. "I'm better than Norm," she says, meaning her father. "He's too senile to hit the hole the first time. Sometimes I think he never learned how. Sometimes I think he just thinks he plays golf and actually goes to the golf course to give his life purpose, a mental golfer."

Molly lets them glance at her. She might at one point confess to an incident, something to explain her hatred, why anger is apparent whenever she speaks of him, the talk of killing him.

The salads come.

The women drink beer in the student pub and make eyes at

men who mean nothing to them. The men, one for each woman out there, represent all the longings they are likely to encounter in life.

Elizabeth imagines that something irrevocable will happen if they go on disobeying the natural order of things, the order they are learning to experience as unnatural.

There are things to look forward to, if not in the way of enlightenment, at least in the way of being included in what is older than any of them, older than Rome, older than Greece, as old as Adam. They can still get married.

Sarah writes letters to Elizabeth from high school, explaining how normal she wants everything to turn out to be, despite difficulty at the beginning.

In Sarah's high school is a boy who loves Sarah for who she is. Has Sarah let him know who she is, as Elizabeth knows Sarah? Sarah barely knows herself, and it is somehow enlightening.

The talk of boys is beginning to bore her.

Elizabeth sees herself as stepping over a ladder. The ladder extends to the lake but does not touch the water. She can swim under it.

Molly Devine is swimming circles around everyone, a shark. Molly is alone in her perceptions, but her perceptions as played out in her limbs, are taking hold of even the feeble. Molly is inventing something, a way to live better.

She swims circles around the homeless. The true homeless she takes to her hips and lips and sucks them. She kisses with her eyes wide open.

Elizabeth wonders whether her grandmother bothered with questions on the chicken farm, or did the land itself give different shape to the questions she was likely to ask, and did the figure of her hungry husband in the doorway, ringing the dinner bell, Mrs. Tory, I'm hungry, come to the kitchen and prepare food for our bodies because food gives meaning and something back for all our labor ... did the figure of the hungry husband and the land behind her stout, young body, did that make enough to lean a life on?

15

Marcia is a teenager in this frame, the same as Elizabeth. Richard, Marcia's paramour, is forty-seven. Marcia smells of good leather from her flight jacket. She disappears with Richard through the hallways of the women's dorm, making sure that no one asks questions.

Besides Marcia and Molly, who at that point is keeping herself simple with a boyfriend from high school, there are Carol and Jennifer and Tawny.

Tawny is not yet dead. She has gone off to work regular hours and not overachieve. Carol is busy in her tiny slot overachieving, overachieving being a language like knitting, something to keep doing to get everything to lie flat.

Carol is full of confusion, from a large, silent, over-achieving family, from a perspective of not knowing how to locate an opening to put a tampon in. Accompanying the overwork and confusion, a misunderstanding about ugliness: Carol lets acne run over her face as a way to be a pure scientist.

Jennifer curls her hair wistfully and washes the basin of each sink in the lavatory before arraying supplies and ointments to wash her face. Jennifer has more gifts than uses for gifts. Her over-involvement with agricultural organizations and fraternity men leave her tongue-tied and lethargic. She marries Chip, a farmer like her father.

Jennifer wants Elizabeth to understand that we return to our beginnings, and not because we couldn't have done something else. She says it at her wedding. Elizabeth realizes that she only shaves for weddings.

16

Elizabeth has no reason to treat Walter badly. She treats him badly out of an inner conviction that men don't know. Elizabeth wants to parry on the lap of one of them all the time: What do you know, man, example of men, tell me what you know.

Walter, who works 200 miles away, knows much that he cannot say, out of an inner conviction that to say anything is to spoil it. Walter rises every day at a certain hour to take the long ride on the

A-train, rocking, rocking, to the end of the line, where he steps out of the car, with much determination, to meet the demands of others.

Elizabeth, as the woman, should do for Walter, as the man. Elizabeth as the woman who is about to board a plane to serve the country should hire someone. But it is not a situation of money. Elizabeth as the young woman set free in a new set of clothing, with an opposite set of principles, should live without a man altogether, and for that reason, Walter seems necessary.

How Walter serves Elizabeth has to do with daily living—joy, guilt, and resentment over suds and folding and ironing clothing. Elizabeth gives Walter language in exchange, little verbal hand-me-downs. She tells Walter that he is benefiting indirectly from a woman club.

Carlos, not Carlos Ramirez with the bad teeth, but Carlos Someone with one gold tooth in the front of his mouth, knows much that he can almost say and much that he can enact. People watch him in his lovely, intricate home and pay him respect to take risks for them. He claims that people do not surround him. He has not invited them.

Carlos will not drink coffee with Elizabeth but will go to the woods in his bare feet and eat mushrooms until the tunnel comes and swallows him, his eyes open.

He speaks briefly of becoming a tube, a worm room.

She lets him in and shuts eyes. He comes hopping into bed at night like a rabbit.

17

Elizabeth calls her father on a Sunday afternoon, from a thousand miles away, to hear of the family. An earthquake shook the hotel room of Mother and Father.

The father says, "An earthquake is like when you are on vacation in the summer, and all the children are running in the hallways toward the swimming pool, but it is your hotel room, too, so the running children are everywhere."

It becomes confusing to remember who is related by bonds and who by marriage. The rules and the brain go on one side, the emotion and actions, the fishing go on one side.

"We used to go fishing."

"Yes, but you never liked worms. You should have gotten more into the worms. We are animals," he says. "We sin because we are animals."

The mother is not seeable. The mother's face is not a pitcher on a table, a ship. The mother is invisible to the eye of the daughter. The separation involves letting the mother lie dead in the imagination. That she would willingly do if it weren't for the mystery it presents. The tiny blockaded image of the childhood with the mother, the adulthood with the father. The forfeiture of time, the ten ungiving mothers. That old home is sealed off, grown over with weeds and exclusions.

18

Elizabeth is getting a little more than she wants out of sexuality. The boy from next door, Kyle, meets her years later on a couch. She has her grip again, this time filled with razors and panties and a toothbrush.

She looks at him after all this time and thinks he is still what she wants in anyone. She says, "I never imagined it would work out, but there's this. I thought it might be possible to meet secretly."

He looks away. "I wasn't blond enough," she says.

He begins to touch her. It looks right, but it feels old. Kyle mentions that some of the girls they used to know have become worn-out women.

Elizabeth empties the grip—they are in her ancestral home—and empties Sarah's suitcase that contains a stuffed animal and lacquered sweatshirts, paint designs of bears and bunnies. She puts lingerie for herself in her sister's suitcase and leaves the animals in a pile on the floor.

Across the street there is a woman on the bed, a dark-haired woman Elizabeth has never seen, Spanish or Italian. The woman is pert in the bed and friendly. She is coaxing and persuasive but not threatening at all.

They could all go to a party, a pig roast. Elizabeth would like that, but she doesn't insist. Kyle would bring her to a party but not stand by her. She is still not girl enough, still too womanly.

19

The voice that says, suddenly, I'm not condemning you, that voice means that someone is condemning her. God as the verbal configuration of all foregoing voices of authority, a composite position of teachers and her mother.

She hears it from other people, the nurse at the health center. The nurse takes two condoms from her jumper pocket and zings them at Elizabeth. "It's your job now. Women must use condoms now, because of AIDS and all the other diseases." The nurse seems unhappy to have to talk about it at all.

Elizabeth tells the nurse that she can't use a condom because she doesn't have a cock.

The nurse looks at her blankly. "You don't understand. The authorities, the doctors and health writers, they say that women must carry condoms now. Either the man wears a condom, or he goes home. If you're at his house, you get out of bed and call a taxi."

Probably the nurse hasn't dealt with many men that way. Probably that is the point that neither one of them is making.

It turns out that Elizabeth's abdominal pains are due to not smoking. The doctor is nice and not condemning. He has daughters himself.

Elizabeth stops at the nurse's station on her way out, carrying several packets of bulking agents, different flavors and brands.

"Constipation, Nurse. I'm constipated because I quit smoking."

The nurse's bun lies like a book on her head. "Smoking isn't good for you," she says.

Carlos never acquires a last name. There are many children in his family, some little ones he has never met. His father came home every three and a half weeks or so, which must be some sort of maximum.

Elizabeth could relive the rest of her life without intercourse. She could live the rest of her life without Schwarzwälder Kirsch Torte. She likes Carlos because his skin is soft, and he has hairs in nice places.

Elizabeth returns to playing piano. It is the central avocational impulse, the basic purposeful activity, besides her job in admissions.

Molly Devine is becoming a professor. Molly would invest in mutuals with an income. At twenty-six, even Molly will not charge investments to her mother's accounts. When Walter suggests to Elizabeth that Molly is unprincipled, Elizabeth points that out. She says, Molly is holding off on securities until she gains her independence.

Molly lets Evan know that she wants gifts of romance. Evan spends one entire paycheck on a blue silk bedroom outfit. Evan works in publishing, academic selection committees, butters the bread of off-brand producers: Heroism and Fraud in Restoration Drama. Whatever people are writing about now. Indians, he says, are pretty big. So are ancient Eastern cultures.

Molly grows bored and moves into a new apartment without him.

The mail lies unsorted on the table of the lit lamp: a letter from Molly's mother, a phone bill, a postcard from Elizabeth of Waikiki. She writes, "Why, Kiki?" referring to a man who wanted Molly. The man didn't know her very well and pledged his love anyway, in the middle of an off-chance restaurant. The next time Molly saw him, he was bearing gifts: roses and the necklace with Kiki on it. Molly had told him her name was Kiki in a burst of mismanagement.

21

Elizabeth loses her sense of having value. Walter isn't waiting at the bus station when she goes to meet him. She imagines several scenarios. Either the bus is early, and she is late, or he is not in yet, and she is early.

She thinks of Walter dead and thinks of cures. There aren't any very good ones. Some people are slightly replaceable, but not Walter.

She thinks of him swinging his legs over the bridge over the river, but he wouldn't do that. Walter acts adjacent. He might be disappointed with her for losing him the way she does, but he would not jump. He would arrange to love someone else eventually, but not jump.

Maybe he is eating a pizza. She hasn't thought of that. Maybe he is doing something alone and not thinking of her. It comforts her to think of Walter having a good time, not sad over her.

She misses him. She knows how to plunge into conversations to take the edge off the missing. Missing Walter is not specific to Walter, but is out of an inner hunger to be felt by him. Someone else could feel her, but he has more patience.

Foraging in many psyches is not an efficient use of time.

22

Elizabeth rises early and puts her feet on the floor and feels with her soles the texture of the wood. She hears the cat yawn, squints and wanders out to the sun, in her bathrobe, and catches a leaf in her teeth. She thinks of hamburger and of Ruby and of bathwater in the same instant.

She slips into the tub and rests her head, lets the soap slip under her back and knees. A good day. Not a sound this early in the morning. Not a rip in paradise.

There has been a long-distance hang-up caller. He has not identified himself except in a moment of feminine gurgling, a swan song, she thinks. Why would someone call her every day, from a long distance, and listen to her say, "Hello," and wait and wait? Who is it?

Some menace or pumpkin from the past, some idler, some coot.

Elizabeth in the aftermath is an idler. No will, no sound, strong and distinct as a birdcall. She thinks of the thousand geese resting in the marsh at Horicon, of their uproarious honking, and of the flirtatious Iranian, calling them not to let down. The geese were stopping on their way south. Not a crime, she thinks, just a different behavior.

Texas Was Better—77

Something has kept her from going to the gods.

A warm shelter on a sea of breeze, a long careful boat of memory and wishing. She holds a version of the world as it means, and that is perhaps natural, not foreseeing.

23

Sarah is not the only one. Sarah is perhaps the cause when the mother tries to call the police, and the father knocks the phone out of her hand. There are words. The father says, "Don't," and the mother says, "I will. I'm taking them away from here."

The mother bars the door with her arms. Sarah and Elizabeth wait on their beds for something right to happen. This is the violent scene associated with the father's drinking. Later Elizabeth decides unfairly that mothers don't call the police because fathers are drinking.

The scene should be horrible, but it is bright. Being in the room with Sarah, the mother holding the men out, gives a safe, light feeling.

The brother breaks the sister's arm and leaves her outside with her foot bleeding from the garden shears.

The mother doesn't call the police. The mother thinks they can stay out of jail, or like Macheath, be freed at the end, when things are at their worst.

Elizabeth can rationalize the twenty boys, but she cannot hold away the blankness or keep the static from descending.

Walter is not the father or the brother. She keeps thinking that the father is the brother and vice versa. Their positions are changing.

She hides under the orange laundry cart. She has a dress on because she can feel the touch of cloth on canvas and the comforting weight of the mother's work above her. The floor in the basement is cold. Her tights hurt.

She knows what the car looks like from underneath, the feeling of the gritty floor on her skin, the seed sacks that lift her. Always pillows are there. This time, seed sacks that she grabs and that carry her to open air, to the empty half of the garage, through the opening to light. She crouches in the grasses around the mailbox and worries that a car will see her hiding.

The brother is in the house. He always is laughing, so it's funny. Seeing him in his underwear, she thinks, He's taking over the house again.

She goes to eat at the neighbors. What they call her, they think she is selfish, a mooch about their food. She is seven or eight or ten. If Jazz Animal is with her, she is seven. Seven is the beginning or the end. Elizabeth tells the neighbor girl who Santa is.

"Remember the animals," her father says. "We are animals and must somehow accept our behavior."

Elizabeth's behavior is scab picking. She returns to scenes of crimes without seeing connotations. The brother was arrested and kicked out in the past.

Elizabeth is not coping today. Elizabeth is not sick. She is too tired to wake up. She can't run because of a paralysis.

She lies in a contorted position on the couch, her arms folded under her like sleeves in a drawer. The pageant is on. The father crouches, his elegant hand draped over his knee. The wave of feeling, the sickness. Gaze squarely on the TV dolls, the United States swimming suits. She thinks, This is responsibility time.

24

She is about to break through to something. She senses it as something approaching, something that she is approaching, since she is moving, and the thing is waiting for her.

At any time, she can look up at the sky and tell where the lake is by watching the clouds. The sky lightens, the clouds make way for lake.

Part of her mind, the front part, has been dim for a long time. Smoky gray, she would call it, smoky bar. That part is changing. She looks up into her mind, and it is milder by degrees every day. The smoke drifts toward the back of her mind, as if she has passed under a storm. Everything coming is light.

The ovaries are cooking, baking up ideas for newborns. She will not lie gladly down and give out children. For children: the fish in the bowl, the sweet tooth, the phone in the bath, and foot massage.

The people downstairs, the people whose building it is, have heard disruptive noises in the night and seen foreign speakers in the lobby. Elizabeth has neglected to lock the door again, and that leaves them in danger.

Most importantly, she forgets to eat enough when Walter is away.

She studies ill-advised behavior as a research method. See which ones laugh and which ones think of sickness. Is it her sickness or their fear? Laughter in others at ill- advised behavior fascinates then sickens her. Satisfaction is an art.

She guards her power, fingers it, resists it, because her people want a mortal. If she felt like it, she could zap them.

Be thankful for what you do have, the voice tells her. Be kind.

Wish for the Left Hand

The woman thought she had no duty except to serve his pierre with her mundo and genie, and when not joined, her duty was to shine in his eyes, to fawn, to accentuate his value by appearing as a precious object to look upon because her duty to write her work mattered less—out of a rival survivalist necessity—or because she knew that to shine her eyes upon him could buy her quiet time to write down her work, her work that showed vehemence. Hardly a soul could pin him for creating the vehemence that found a streamule to her pen if she wrote on paper or a fanjet to her keyboard, typing very quickly and exactly and satisfyingly in print, not cursive, printing very quickly using eight fingers and two thumbs, the left thumb idle but prepared and doing nothing except yielding during the typing procedure, the left thumb guidant or conversant with the other thumb, with the balance in the wrist, with the rest—woe it is the duty of the right thumb to type the space, leaving no duty for the left thumb but to be there. If she were to lose a manual digit, it is the left thumb that could go with ease and not injure her typing, her vehemence, not distress her for writing purposes—she could do without distress were she to be missing her left thumb. Her shining eyes would seem piteous without her thumb, but he would sometimes forget it, her missing thing, her finger, an exaggeration of their other worries, cut off on a windshield wiper, or the horrors and the honors.

Travel

I texted a wickety-split, tax-declaring New York-based international escort, a moonlighting, all-pro Kit, whose day job on Wall Street yields no bonus. Is Christmas when bonuses are paid? At MadHat, work is not paid except to the attorney and member elites. I did not catch a steamer to Asheville, as Mina Loy seeking Arthur Cravan, after Conrad missed his New York performance, but I did ride to Georgia and find a stand of giraffes.

Hogging the Lady

This is the hardest of the stories. This is the story that belongs in its place. This is the story that takes second place. It is the story that follows its master. It is the story that grows old. It is the story for a season, for fall.

Which door did she slip in, in her torn fishnet stockings and faux leather skirt, brown, her mascara falsely applied, her vacant blouse in need of hitching. She was not the usual member of the band, not the girl nextdoor, not next to any door, not a regular housekeeper or woman. She was a ditch digger, a pied, circular piper, a mouse hugger.

I took her to be the last of her generation. She seemed drunk without eating. She seemed ashamed without sin. She seemed cursed without a family. She seemed as though she had planned a porkchop for the boys and girls of Tallahassee. She seemed to believe that she had roped a strong pony. In the first movement her dance looked lonely and lame. Then she got up on the stage and tried to kiss the front man. He didn't want to kiss her at first, but when he did, something magical happened, something tender.

She got down off the stage and put down her riding crop. She started loving the air. She started singing in her voices. She started dancing. She whistled a bar of Dixie then she sallied north. She swiveled her legs and her arms, looking much like a 44-year-old rodeo worker on the floor at Christopher's, but she was at the Turfside. Everyone wanted to dance with her, a face she well knew, but that did not seem to be the reason to dance for her. She danced, it seemed, so that others would dance, too, and they did.

Dumb Luck

Radio

It is a long morning that begins with a hymn on the radio. She turns in her sleep, roused awake by the singer's training.

Her boss calls during lunch hour

To a pedestrian crossing at 14th Street: "Am I facing uptown or downtown?" "Up," the pedestrian says stopping. Directions and hybrids blur in the mind while rotating. Apple stand, mint, wheat grass juice, rutabaga, tie-dyeds. Amish wagon to the curb. Sunshine breaks an egg over Phillips Ambulatory. Tall—for walking—espresso on ice. Lunch crowd milling. 9.8 per cent out of work. Telephone snapshot of flower stand.

Telephone rings: Señor Carlisle.

"Hello," Señorita Mill pretends not to know.

"Hell-o-ah," he mocks her.

"Stop," she says and corrects: "Hell-o."

"Where are you?"

"Union Square."

"Is it raining?"

"Sunny."

"Pick up a Post and a pair of green apples."

Miss widow

Mill takes her assignment and heads with it toward Broadway to walk past the windows of discount shoes. She thinks Carlisle lives in the Shoe Box District, but she hasn't said it. She asked for leave to visit a club in the Meat Packing District, and Carlisle said he'd send her to the Diamond District if she wasn't careful. She imagined riding the subway alone to the Diamond District to size her engagement ring, but nothing came of it besides banter about the burden of money. "The Statue of Liberty is the color of money," he told her on a Saturday. Apples at the Farmers' Market are the color of dairy barns not green. Carlisle means "Granny Smiths" from New Zealand.

Mill picks the firmest green apples from the bin at Modern Gourmet. The deli is out of the Post, so she buys Raisin Bran as a joke at her expense. The shopkeepers are not fluent in the vocabulary of groceries: Motrin for margarine. All the service workers are fluent in the ways to pay. Currency is universal. The owner's wife takes her dollars and returns her change. Mill puts the coins in her pocket to give to the man outside.

A new pair of glasses

"Miss Mill," Umberto greets her when she gets to Carlisle's building.

She lifts the bag of groceries over the counter. "Good noon, Umberto. This is for Mr. Carlisle."

"You're not going up?"

"I have rounds," she says.

"What do I tell him?"

"That I have rounds."

Umberto stares at her hopefully.

"Errands," she says.

"Work for Mr. Carlisle?"

"Yes," she says.

"I'll tell him. Good afternoon, Miss Mill."

"Goodbye, Umberto."

Mill passes Il Cantinori on her way to University Place. Its french doors are open, and lunchers sit at tables half inside, half outside, sipping wine and eating dull bread.

At Devonshire Optical, the bell klingels as she opens the door. She fishes in her red wallet for her prescription. She wants green frames. She peers through the cases. There is one green pair. The clerk lets her try them on, but they do not suit her face. She sees a light brown pair.

"These," she says to the clerk. The clerk sits with her at a fitting table to take adjustments then writes her name and address and telephone number on an index card.

"We'll call when they're ready," the clerk says.

"I'll wear these until then," Mill says. Mill paid $3 on Minnesota Care for the wire pair. In Minnesota, she wears them for driving and at the theater. In the city, she wears them to see to the end of the block and discern faces on *Law & Order*. When Carlisle saw them, he told her to get new ones.

At the drugstore

Mill puts the receipt for the glasses in her wallet and leaves the store, bell klingeling. She crosses the street to Whitney Chemists. The bell rings.

She fishes in her wallet for Carlisle's prescription.

"Ten minutes," the pharmacist tells her.

"I'll wait," Mill says and sits in the solitary chair.

She fishes in her satchel for a plain white envelope, a pen, and a roll of stamps. She writes Carlisle's address on the envelope and puts the receipt for her glasses in it: $386.

"Here it is," the pharmacist tells her. "$127."

"Do you have his insurance card?" Mill says.

"Viagra isn't covered. We called."

Mill gives the pharmacist her credit card, signs, then tucks the receipt in the mailer.

When she gets to Carlisle's building, she gives Umberto the packet from Whitney Chemists.

"Thanks, Umberto."

"You're welcome, Miss Mill. Still working?"

"Still working," she says.

Mill drops the envelope in the mailbox at Broadway then walks the three blocks home.

In for the night

The telephone rings: Señor Carlisle.

"Hello," Señorita Mill pretends not to know.

"Where are you?" Carlisle says.

"At home," Mill tells him.

"What are you wearing?"

Mill is silent.

"What are you wearing?" Carlisle asks again.

"A skirt!" Mill says.

"The skirt I bought you?" Carlisle says.

"A skirt my mother gave me," Mill says, "and a lightweight cardigan."

"The brown skirt?" Carlisle says.

"It's beige," she tells him.

"What are your plans?"

"I have no plans," Mill says.

"You're in for the night?" Carlisle insists.

"I'm in for the night," she says.

"You're safe?" he asks.

"Perfectly," she says.

"This is New York City," he reminds her.

"I'm safe in my apartment," she says.

"Your door is locked?"

"Yes," she says.

"You have plenty of food? What are you having for dinner?"

"Sandwiches," she says.

"What kind of sandwich?"

"Grilled cheese with salad," she says.

"And you have shopped?"

"Yes," she says.

"Umberto said you came in twice this afternoon—that you were 'working.' I said that unless you were in the upstairs room that you were bamboozling him. He didn't know the word 'bamboozle.' "

"I'll explain last weekend's overtime then," she says.

"Define bamboozle," Carlisle says.

"Gyp," Mill says.

"Look it up," Carlisle says. "Read it to me."

Mill goes to her computer. "1. cheat somebody: to trick or deceive somebody through misleading statements or falsehoods. 2.

perplex somebody: to make somebody confused."

"I bamboozled Umberto," Carlisle proffers.

"Yes," she says.

He can read her thoughts

Mill knits Carlisle a pullover evenings. The pullover is dark brown with a beige v- at the neck and stripe at the cuff. Carlisle does not deserve a pullover. Carlisle deserves a lump in the head for his incessant phone calls and demands. A man ought to buy his own newspaper, she thinks,m ought to buy his aunt a birthday card. He ought to move his chaise longue and see to it when he needs towels. Carlisle hired her to keep books, yet the labor is indivisible. She feels indentured, not like a service worker. The service workers have position and pride. She has no pride. She has little pride. Carlisle's idea of service would shape a Founding Father. Smoke rises from her tender temple. She puts on water for tea.

"Miss Mill," Carlisle begins when she answers the phone.

"Yes," Mill says. She wraps the teapot in a crisp dishcloth.

"Your service is unimpeachable," he says.

"It's nothing," Mill says. He can read her thoughts after hours when all the shops are closed. He can read her thoughts at a distance of city blocks. He can read her thoughts over the din of books on the bedside table. He can read thoughts she filters with J. S. Bach.

Cognates in the Post

In the morning Mill arrives at Carlisle's suite with Post in hand. The Post lies ravaged on the empty desk. Her chair is parked in the center of the room, wheels askew. (She leaves it neatly positioned under her desk with its wheels pointed toward the wall.) The spare chair is in its usual position tucked under the empty desk. She inclines it toward her desk then straightens the wheels of her chair by sliding it along the lines in the Persian rug and sits.

The telephone rings: Señor Carlisle.

"Hello," Señorita Mill pretends not to know.

"See page 7," he says.

Mill opens the clean copy of the Post to page 7. "Baseball topper," she reads, "tests plus for 'roids."

" 'Zat one 'roid or two?" Carlisle says.

"The article doesn't go into it," Mill says.

"Spell hemorrhoid," Carlisle says.

"H-e-m-m," Mill says.

"Look it up," he says.

Mill wakes the computer. "H-e-m-o-r-r-h-o-i-d," she says.

"Baseball topper's 'hoids test-us," Carlisle proffers.

"Calumny," Mill says, flanking her hair.

Carlisle is silent.

"I hired you to follow stock reports," he says. "I keep you because you know the word 'calumny.' Read the definition."

Mill toggles the mouse, "1. defamation: the making of false statements about somebody with malicious intent. 2. defamatory statement: a slanderous statement or false accusation.

"15th century. From Latin calumnia or false accusation (also the source of English challenge), from calvi 'to deceive.'"

Talk of the weather

The rain changes the shapes of trees. It changes the buildings, though not, she thinks, this building. This building stays dry and firm. Mill takes out her magnifying glass and begins to harvest statistics.

The telephone rings: Carlisle.

"Hello," Mill says.

"You want to know how bad it is?" he says.

"It doesn't look all bad," she says.

"It's a black cloud over a picnic before it rains. It's a jammed pistol. It's a dictionary with half the letters removed."

"It's a tornado that hits your barn not your house," Mill says as he hangs up.

Mill pans the indices for gold. "One 'roid or two¿" plays in her mind like a strain from a musical. Couple of street paranoids, it says. "'Zat one 'noid or two¿" she rehearses. "When 'noids talk, money listens."

One male ape to another: "Is that a butt or a breastplate through the trees¿"

The phone rings: Carlisle.

"What is O-I-D¿" Mill says.

"Oxford Indiana Dictionary," he says.

"The suffix is from Greek," Mill says, "and means 'like, resembling, or related to' from eidos: form or shape."

"Original Issue Discount," he says, "or H-O-T."

"What's H-O-T¿" she says.

"You," he says. "It's Hell on Taxes."

"A porn koan," she says.

"Hah!" he says. T

he goose escapes the glass.

Time tells her

Mill attended the University of Minnesota in the 1980s. She majored in English. One of her friends from childhood, Nancy O'Reilly, acted as if she had outgrown Mill by college. Mill saw Nancy O'Reilly days in Coffman Union reading psycholinguistics textbooks. Mill sat tables away reading Donne or Pope or Dryden or Swift but not the Romantics. Mill knew her own heart too little, the result of having a formal mother. If Nancy O'Reilly had stayed her friend, if their intellects had banded together, Mill might have realized she wanted a career in banking.

Had she realized she wanted a career in banking, she might have met her husband. Had she met her husband, she might have had children. Mill became an office worker with progressive responsibilities and static paycheck, and Nancy O'Reilly went on to earn a Ph.D. in linguistics. Mrs. Mill got a thank you note from Mrs. O'Reilly after

Nancy O'Reilly had become Nancy O'Reilly-Kemp, though Nancy O'Reilly hadn't invited Mill to the wedding. Later Mrs. Mill learned from Mrs. O'Reilly at the grocery store the O'Reilly-Kemps had two children.

Mill wrote, "Bookkeeping is to the Romantics as Teheran is to Carter," and sent it to Carlisle's blind box ad.

Interview

It was Mill's dumb luck that Carlisle's favorite president was Jimmy Carter. At least, that's what he said when he phoned her mother's house in Wayzata. That and his mother had grown up in St. Paul.

His mother's father had given him a dictionary that had belonged to Mark Twain. The dictionary was signed by Twain and lying in a safety deposit box in Connecticut. Carlisle had read it in its entirety the summer after boarding school.

Carlisle told her he was glad that a Minnesota gal had answered the ad, and, "not just any farm-fed," he said, "but a gal with English and a little economics under her belt."

"We belong together," he said that first phone call, "as John Stuart Mill and Thomas Carlyle."

"I read an article about their fire in The New Yorker," Mill acknowledged.

"The New Yorker delivers out in Wayzata?" Carlisle said.

"Their subscription center is in Red Oak, Iowa," Mill said.

"Boone," Carlisle corrected her.

As a child, another child had called Mill "Little Miss Know-It-All" and "nigger lips" on the same day. That child was a woman by then, a divorcing and foreclosed woman with two children and a married black lover.

He heralds newsworthy deaths

Telephone rings: Carlisle.

"Hello," Mill pretends not to know.

"Are you sitting down?" Carlisle asks.

"I'm pacing," she says.

"Why do you pace so much?" he asks.

"It's exercise," she says.

"It's a lunatic asylum in there," he says. Mill's ancestors were more stable than Carlisle's.

"The market is down," he says, but that's not why he's calling. "Are you sitting down?" Then, as is his custom, Carlisle reads the Times obituaries page to her.

"It's curtains for Curtin," he summarizes before reading the text. "Scholar of the slave trade dead at 87."

"Bogle bit it," he says.

"Founder of Vanguard?" Mill asks.

"Bob of the Ventures," he says. "You're too young to remember Hawaii Five-0."

"I am not!" Mill protests foolishly, tired of hearing him say she is too young to remember things. "I washed dishes to it."

Mill learns more about life from Carlisle's daily slog through the obituaries than she likes to admit. She pretends to an estranged discomfort at the thought or mention of death— shudders on cue at it—but she is in fact glad that people die: and not only people but all living things. Mortality is the universal sign that democracy exists outside its documents, that it has a natural basis, she thinks.

A motto for love

Before Mill moved to New York to work for Carlisle, she lived with her mother to spare expenses. One night Mill asked idly over supper what love is, not believing her mother would know.

Her mother said, "Many people live without it."

Mrs. Mill did not seem to wonder about love after Mr. Mill had died nor during forty years of practical marriage. Yet Mrs. Mill knew enough, perhaps all there was to know about love.

Mill set her heart on living with it.

Mill lives graciously without love in the 00s. A student of modernism, the 80s were her 20s, the 90s her 30s, the auts her 40s.

Her lifetime is an odometer reset to zero. She is a car parked at auction, an antique or classic, not a dragster. She is a beauty restored to a season, not a hot virgin or spinster, but an old maid with a lesbian's timing. Bidders ignore her or come in low.

There was an ice storm not a hurricane when she lived in Texas.

Men gently used her to make love without commitment in her 20s. In her 30s, the men were more vigorous, and she once called the police, believing police were the bureau to care. The policemen stood at her apartment door with sheepish blue eyes and bulges at the hip. She hoped no one would fire a gun. One of the officers said, "Let sleeping dogs lie," while the man most presumed innocent by the jury said, "Don't lie to the officers." Mill thanked them. The next day she resigned her job and packed suitcases and boxes for Minnesota. The men were all cowards, Mrs. Mill said, and, "Justice has been served."

La discrimination positive

Mill sits down when Carlisle calls to ask why she isn't married.

"Rig-a-marole," she says.

"It's heating up," Carlisle says. "Look it up."

"It's an alternate spelling," Mill says, feeling apologetic for her one-more syllable, as when she says real-a-tor and Viag-a-ra. "I saw Niagara when I was three," she says.

"Three is too young," Carlisle says.

"I was in high school when the Equal Rights Amendment didn't pass—the Supreme Court said then that women are 'people' under the Constitution—a lot of people were listening," Mill says. "I thought it meant I would become an 'adult person' not a 'woman.' All we got was 'privacy' amid street protests and religious cantilevering over abortion."

"We are all people of color," Carlisle says.

"Some people are slower of color than others," Mill says.

She speaks to her mother on Tuesdays, but today her mother is in Eau Claire with her garden journey group.

Her mother knows that Mill has met Carlisle in person, but certain others in Minnesota suspect that she has never even seen him. They quiz her during return trips on his appearance: Is he tall, broad, handsome, good-natured, good-looking, older, younger, available?

"He's my boss," she says, or "he is he," when cornered.

Carlisle asks for discretion in relating details of her position to anyone except her mother, whom he has judged (without meeting) to be of the older generation, from the set who survived the Great Depression and World Wars, who preserves homegrown tomatoes, who is old school. Mrs. Mill is all that, and she is also a *modern*.

Mill misses the wildlife of her home in Wayzata: the rabbits at the birdfeeder, the deer in the woods, the gardens and wild leeks. She misses the moths and butterflies, the frogs that climb and toads that crawl. She misses Tilly Artaud, an American toad who sat at Mill's glass door every midnight for a summer, as if she had swallowed a Timex watch battery. She misses her cat, The Doctor: his bushy gray tail and Roman nose, his pacing the hallways at night as if carrying transcripts of her speeches to Congress.

Carlisle has urged her to get a dog to walk in the morning. If she gets a dog, his name will be "Johann." If she doesn't get one, she'll consider a bird.

Truck

Mill rolls her chair under the desk and turns out the light.

The phone rings: Carlisle.

Mill answers in the dusk.

"I talked to your mother," Carlisle says.

"She's in Eau Claire," Mill says, not bothering to turn on the light.

"She's back," Carlisle says. "I asked her why you left Texas, and she said, 'Truck.'"

"She's flirting with you," Mill says. "I told you she is a modern."

"What is 'truck' in her lexicon?" Carlisle says.

Mill turns on the light and budges the mouse. " 'Keep on truck-ing'," Mill says, " 'to carry on with work or life in a cheerful and re-laxed way, in spite of problems (informal).' "

"Your mother is a contemporary of Jerry Garcia, Robert Hunter, and The Grateful Dead," Carlisle says.

"Truck that hauls or carries," Mill says.

"I get the idea you didn't 'fall off the turnip truck,' " Carlisle says. "Or the 'Swedish carrot' truck to be German about it," he adds, referring to last week's discussion of "rutabaga."

" 'Truck' is archaic for barter," Mill says. "That is probably the sense she means."

"What sort of truck was it in Texas?" Carlisle says.

"Small as truck goes," Mill says. "Smaller than a full-size pick-up."

"If full-size pick-up means you killed someone?" Carlisle says.

"No, if eighteen-wheeler means someone else did," Mill says. "It wasn't my truck."

"Whose truck was it?"

"Dean's," Mill says.

"Go on," Carlisle says.

"Dean is my former boyfriend," Mill says.

"Dean is his last name?" Carlisle says.

"Dean is his middle name," Mill says.

"Did he hurt you?" Carlisle asks.

"If by hurt, you mean dismayed, disappointed, or chagrined, yes," Mill says.

"I mean *hit*," Carlisle says. "Did he hit you?"

"He hit the wall next to my bed," Mill says.

"Are you still in love with him?" Carlisle says.

"It was last century," Mill says. "I'm in love with The Doctor as I told you."

"Whose doctor?" Carlisle says. "Your doctor?"

"The Doctor," Mill says, "my cat."

The phone rings: Carlisle.

"Good evening," Mill says.

"Where are you?" he says.

"At home," she says.

"Are you in for the night?" he says.

"Yes," she says.

"Have you thought about the coming year twenty-ten?" Carlisle says.

"Is twenty-ten what we'll call it?" Mill says.

"Your voice sounds sexy when you're sleepy," he says. "Look it up."

"It isn't in the dictionary," she says after a pause. "It was a science fiction novel and film. The census is next year and the winter Olympics in Vancouver."

"Twenty-ten will be a good year," he says.

"Everyone is hoping," she says. "People say this was a bad decade due to the War."

"Obama won," Carlisle says.

"Yes," she says, "Obama will be President in twenty-ten."

"Miss Mill will be Mrs. Carlisle," he says.

"You borrow trouble," she says.

"I eschew borrowing," he says. "It's a fair topic."

"We're not equal," she says.

"Look it up," he says.

"Es-choo," she says, "sounds like a sneeze. I prefer es-skew, but it isn't listed. It comes from old German meaning shy."

"We are equal under the law," he says.

"Equal in legal contexts," she says. "Otherwise it means identical."

"You're sure?" he says.

"That is what it says right here," she says. "I thought I would call my lawyer," he says. "You call your lawyer, and we'll sit down and hash it out and come up with a prudent agreement."

"I never wanted a big church wedding," Mill says. "I lost my belief in God early. It was like losing my virginity by falling off a bike or horse. I lost connection with God when I hit the ground. I got back on the bike or horse and rode away, but I was godless."

"Religion is the source of true fiction," he says.

"I feel like a mail-order bride from Canada," she says.

Denouement

She imagines Carlisle in a wheelchair. One of her friends in Minnesota said, "Is he in a wheelchair? Is that why you aren't talking? Is he old and in a wheel chair?"

Mill imagines him in a wheelchair; she imagines him standing miraculously to touch her hair. She imagines him old and miraculously turning fifty. She imagines the denouement.

"Come up and see me sometime," she drawls. "Is that a pistol in your pants or are you just happy to see me?"

When the doorman rings, Mill remembers Carlisle can read her thoughts. "Let him up," Mill says. She is wearing an African kaftan and briefs and a bra under it. She is glad her legs are waxed, her hair and nails are fresh. She slips on flat sandals and pulls a brush through her hair. She douses herself with Dior, leaves the door ajar, and waits.

Carlisle steps inside the apartment as if he were there to build it, mysteriously raising his foot as if clearing a stone fence. He is wearing a black suit and hat.

Mill blushes as if she has nothing to hide.

"Come here," Carlisle says. He locks his fingers behind her neck and pulls her to his mouth. They fall into a bookshelf. "You're not getting out of this."

"I quit my job," she mumbles.

"You quit your job in twenty-ten," he says.

Irish Salad

Scandinavians settled in Minnesota because it resembled Scandinavia. This morning I vomited salad I ate last night at an Irish pub. The salad was called "chop chop." I paid $19 for the food and two beers. I met the owner whom we help to become rich with our simple appetites. We were rich farmers from Scotland and Sweden. He is Irish but unlike other Irish-American people I know, he is from Ireland. He is red-headed, swarthy and muscular. He imported the mahogany bar from Dublin. I wish my simple appetites might feed two in our decision instead of helping him if he is a tax-evader like so many of the restaurateurs. Asian restaurants serve vegetables with love. Overnight, I felt drunk, as if headed for hangover, but I hadn't drunk enough to cause it. What caused it? Superstitions dialed in sleep. Today I was thick with religious devotion. I had thought about delicious corned beef and cabbage not to be served at that public house on St. Patrick's Day. I wanted the Irish of Binghamton, the fire department, and the Irish of literature to comfort me. To avoid this drunkenness not caused by drinking. I was so balanced before it was revealed. Ladylike reserves be restored to me.

Two Hundred Fifty

Sometimes I think we are in it all together, responsible to each other and for what happens to one another. We can prevent suicides. Other times I think this thinking is jaded, that having strange longings for world peace is unjustified. Happier and more optimistic people than I feel we are not in it for peace, not responsible for war or suicide. One million people die every year at their own hand, the hand that swallows the pills or plies a knife or loops a noose or turns on the gas. It amounts to more deaths than homicide and war combined. For every person who dies alone that way, another twenty try. An attempt that leads to death is called "completed." I think it affects rent. The dead guy is not the bad guy, the only bad guy in a serene film about beauty, the living not the good guys on a team that wins at war. He is in his own category. He carries a name or label. He has a "profile" under law. In China it's women. Some people are against fear. I am more against hate than against love. Someone will try to tell you that love is a sickness. Someone is always diagnosing.

I walked and then I ran. I was in the woods on a paved path and couldn't tell how long a block was: I just ran from tree to tree, blue racing line to blue racing line, thinking of kilometers.

Primary Creative

1. Cyril in Texas

The dead characters lay in a pool of their own divination.

Carly, the troll, had drowned Suzy, the shrimp. Fingers, the magic cop, formed a union to protect anonymous achievement. Cyril spent two nights in the heart of a novel— and really it should have been more since Cyril was the better sort of character, left out by these other sorts in their greed and lust for attention, innovation, and star standing. Kitty used Cyril dryly to stop her vagina from atrophying.

Aghast, Kitty had learned from her mother that her—meaning Kitty's own—vagina would atrophy one day, too, and to stop wasting her every day with her old person's fixations on the past and on problems in society. Where had she—meaning Kitty's mother—gone wrong? She had had one of the first breast implants to encourage sexuality in all her daughters. She had dated men after her separation from Kitty Durango's dad. She had sold one of her houses to pay for Kitty's college degree. She had attended all of Kitty's stage performances—theater in the best sense of the word is what she had urged in her and failing that, to thrive. Despite all this, Kitty had gotten stuck thinking of her ninth year.

What had happened that day in school had been really disgraceful; okay, Kitty could see her own part in it. Nonetheless, what happened should not have happened to her or any child: a mission. Kitty had no goals for having children of her own—she did not want to have them nor even not-want to have them. She wanted a soul mate. Ha! She would invent a surgery for that, add a dna-connected magnet to a major bone, the breast plate or a rib or hip bone, the pelvic area, call it a soul detector. That would show who's whose boss around town, especially if she had one of the first ones, her own first boss or a first soul detector— she would know what to do with one of those. Soul detectors would not cause cancer or the fear of cancer in newcomers. There were all brainless masters in the club scene.

Carol was her only find who did not know about those clubs,

so Carol was an added benefit, a safety feature, even a soother after such long lines of nights. Carol never heard anyone talk about clubs. She liked talk of religion that had little bearing on religion. She liked disappearing into elevators when they were swallowing huge clumps of people or being her own self-contained neurobump— (how could the nature camera tell a male neurobump in a seersucker suit coat from a female neurobump in a hooded sweater vest?)—as she was being swallowed singly by a slow-moving elevator in a parking ramp. If there were one place it seemed easy to take the stairs, parking ramps were it, a topic with significance. Carol failed to tell Kitty, Carly, Suzy, Cyril, Fingers, or Dude, her boyfriend, about her world's most private moments spent in public, paying a visit to the doctor. Doctors were educated, and these other people were barely educated. Doctors had nice numbers and billing systems that kept track of a schedule for her, that kept her on time, a date, and focused on a body part. Today it was a varicosity in her shin. She didn't like moves anymore, had given them up. She liked very little about many days without disliking the idea of a typical "day."

Dude imagined Carol at the warehouse and thought of her being injected with semen over and over and nixed it, so it was left up to him. Kitty Durango mentioned that Carol might like nice caresses from strangers and acquaintances, especially the women, knowing Carol only as a safe find and not as Dude probably knew her. No, Dude said, adding that Carol had had sex with her own father (Carol did not know he had told her friends that: IT WAS NOT ACTUALLY TRUE, and she might never have a chance to clear the air; it was useless for them to guess at other people's conversations). Carol was following a doctor's protocol that bore no discoveries, so Kitty desisted, mostly because other people were not her problem.

The courtly group liked sex to be towering over other people with rifles; Carol liked it on her back without clothes. They would not have been near her that way. She had never seen Dude with a rifle. The two of them had sex nude as if in one little railroad flat, like fine Traditionalists. Kitty and Dude never knew that certain people who had befriended Carol, not Carly and Suzy but people like them, had ordered doctors for Carol during the finale of an upset, to see, to see what doctors would do to her, to see what doctors, in fact, do. It was like a celibacy to sell her so dry, and it was stupid of Carol (Corolla, Cadillac) not to realize it. Henceforth, she dealt quietly in varying forms of mixed obedience as if she had not "gotten it."

Carly (Corona) and Suzy (Pilsner Urquell) brought their best -xist rifles to Fingers for his tax company.

2. Blind Date

Kitty Durango's dad was the law doctor, doctor of law, law-man, legal adversary, law specialist, the one who knew, ask Kitty's dad. Kitty will make an appointment to ask her dad; her dad will know what to tell Fingers about his tax company—whether to go not-for- profit or trade, small, a personal fund-raiser, levying taxes from home, from his rental cottage (Fingers loved that house against odds of vying developers zeroing in on his neighborhood) for private causes; these were formerly public concerns, topics, such as "the road bill"; now no one had kept up an interest in it. Kitty Durango's friends only wanted art, what Kitty's dad had predicted in 1977 with a telescopic intelligence. Kitty said, "not Fingers," who still liked art. At least one of them was moving on it, a business to raise taxes.

Carol cheered up just thinking of industry! This is not a good sign, Kitty realized, to let Carol cheer up too much about things that don't concern her. Keep Carol out of it, busy with doctor visits. At least Carol kept her business to herself, something Kitty liked about her.

Dude had met Kitty on a blind date—Kitty had put herself up to it, a checklist item. She was not actually looking. Dude thought Kitty was spectacular, like a wild monk, like a Manx cat, like a free catholic. Kitty was episcopalian at her wedding to HERO. She still refused to say his name to the new gang. His name was bleeped. His father was a MAJOR FIGURE, all right. Had not worked out in his case, okay, a goofball. Carol had thought that Kitty's Mr. 'hmm hmm' was very handsome. Once she even sat with him at a stage rehearsal. "You are not allowed to speak to him," Kitty dragged them into it, then out of it. HERO was Kitty's ex-husband. Kitty was very sensitive. After her blind date with Dude, a find, no sex, her fingers (Kitty applied her agile fingers to give him a preview or trailer—a trailer! Dude cried out in the car—Thanks!—for coming attractions, he added)—Kitty referred him to Carol. Carol thought Dude was handsome. Dude, now rerouted, was happy just to be there, to be somewhere! With such nice people. (Interesting occasions).

Kitty landed Cyril on a terrace, where he had gone at her urging to steal carnations from a vase. Green carnations. She wanted one pink one and one white one. When they found them, all the way at the far end of the balcony, she unzipped him, the green carnation jammed between his teeth.

Carly, Suzy, Fingers. There is not a possibility of couples here. Carly jeered at couples. Suzy handled the curtains like a game show, like a showroom hostess. They had been strippers, but that was all together ordinary. They had not saved up any money. People thought they had made so much money. People thought $3,000 was so much money for a week of work. It's not that much, Carly countered. Not a base or let them bring a base in. Fingers had basic white hair—like the colonel. Fingers needed a computer to run his tax company. He had a computer but needed a different computer. Carly and Suzy could put up flyers.

3. Rut

French citizens. The friends were all citizens of a half-assed France. The friends were all half-assed citizens of a French stance. Carol was more American, more eggnog, more cream-of-wheat. She represented dull victory. The others, the main hand of them— five or six!—counted up to a contingency. They were essentially legal. There was sex, all legal. There were partners, and those were legal. Legal if they moved in together, not true with the gays, but gays were more used to it. Gays were in favor of interviewing because they were newer, but not new like immigrants, new like shoe hat or blessed by an era. The group were not married yet. They ought to get married: Kitty Durango will quick marry Cyril after quick divorcing HERO (humph harumph, his real name). Carol will marry Dude who never married Cheryl who had their son. Carol will help raise the boy. Fingers will not marry—and here is how he would like it—both Suzy and Carly. He wants a pair of them: not the one but the two. Not two wives, but a pair of yet-sisters. A pair of skates. One pair of not-friends, his real running shoes. Call the legislator.

Carol is blessed with two hundred acquaintances from towns around the country. She interprets the gays to the straights: They are all nice people, she says. They want what other people want, only they believe they're better at relationships. It's based on hard work and trying. Carol okays Fingers but doesn't get Carly and Suzy. They are two-colored, orange and white, a cookie split down the middle—a white Halloween treat. Treat them right! she would offer as a suggestion, but Fingers already treats them kindly; the two girls don't want more than they are getting, but they want these basics to continue. They want more of some.

Once married, the two new pairs plus the three others, who aren't married would win up the town. The married pairs—Kitty and Cyril particularly—would trump Fingers and his ho-hum business plan involving two women without a legal wife.

Carol and Dude would raise his son with Cheryl—"Jesus H. Cheryl" Dude called his former non-wife once, so that Carol checked her flags: Is it sacrilege to call someone Jesus? The son was the actual one. Benny was such a good name for a son, Carol told him. Benny was in third grade. He was frankly horrible at school. Carol would need to tutor him for Cheryl, whom she supposed was not equipped. Dude would welcome the assistance but not this year. They would get married but not go ahead of the pack. Carol and Dude already seem married, Carly said ruefully.

There was a song, an old gay tune, a real silencer among the old—who were all wildly against gay people, and these were people living in homes and hitting at each other with canes. I warn you, get away from me, old man, the song went. The people said it was a song by an old woman to her husband.

Dreams-in-progress

I noticed that on nicotine patch I dreamt of celebrities and sex. These were men who knew me in the dreams but not in life. All of them were extremely famous, except Dan Fogerty, who used to be more famous and who kissed me like a teenager. Redford came in a limo. With Dylan the embrace was of friendship for my real friend, Jack. A team of reggae journalists played and an unknown man came for me after work in a kilt.

Perhaps it's due to Wellbutrin — who knows? — that I dream now of celebrities I have met and who might argue against it, their fame, as a false claim, one that means (since no one besides poets and students, colleagues and friends knows them) a familiarity related to but unlike widespread fame.

I walked into a party. Men I'd heard of and more than "heard of" were there, whose veiled, intimate thoughts revealed in pages of risky avant-garde literature I had read. I was wearing new shoes that were a half size too small. My feet had grown from pounding the pavement looking for someone. The homelessness had broken open in me without interrupting shelteredness.

I had slept alone with a dry head in a soft bed. It was as if I had always slept that way. I might have resorted to holding a stuffed animal. There was a reason for this celibacy but it was not religion or disease. It was society. I had exceeded a limit placed on all of us — how many hands we are to hold before picking the hand we most wish to hold for life. I had thought it was a numeral but it was a resonance, one that happens early then recurs.

I hit upon it with a musician, a famous man married for decades, a soul already spoken for, enough. I was poor (despite my shelter) and I had learned that "poor" is different from "broke" which didn't apply to all poor people. "Broke" described the nouveau poor. And "clarity" I suggested we use when "enough" had been reached.

I dreamt in three dreams that we were at a poetry reading and at two A.A. meetings. In the second dream of the meetings the married musician suggested that I read seafaring novels to help the alcoholic I had next met. The alcoholic had rejected A.A. as brainwashing.

Enough, enough, enough, but it wasn't yet enough: clarity in action.

In the earlier dream about the meetings — the rooms change — I am bottomless under the table and must cross the room to find pants. My fat shows, fat that wasn't there when he met me, vantage he would not have seen.

In the dream of the poet there is a wide sweeping lawn, and we flirt, but it is or is not the same thing, and we have no words for it: "legislation," "negotiation," "foundation." I collide with him on a hill and knock him over. I recircle the hill to see him but by then he is busy.

Earlier, not ten years of it, I had walked into Keillor's bookstore and the word "clarity" was written across a banner under the ceiling. Enough, I was thinking, but the furtive position of one seeking clarity or enough, quietly or alone, was barely enough when I couldn't see those brown eyes or pass a guess.

Chinese

Brian sits with his hands under the table, fingers upturned like legs of dead beetles. He'd like to say something to Brenda, but she moved her chair away—the leg of the table was between her legs. It would be better if she would scoot towards him, even if he had to move closer to Mrs. Benjamin. The distance between them is disconcerting. Only their butter plates meet. Brenda rearranged them to give Laura more room. Laura is at the end of the table with almost no space to plant her elbows. Girls Laura's age plant their elbows in public, whenever they can, as an act of defiance. Mrs. Benjamin can't see Laura's elbows or her dress shoes kicked off under the table; otherwise there would be Young Lady This and Young Lady That. How people continue to be families Brian doesn't know.

"Brian, would you like some shrimp?" Mrs. Benjamin's face is too near his. He leans to one side, toward the vacant space. Brenda is eating shrimp almost daintily. Really, she's picking at it, unconvinced she wants to eat it. He knows her. The side of her head is waiting for him. He must answer Mrs. Benjamin. Over my dead body, he thinks. Brenda's hair twitches.

"Okay," he says.

"It's very good," says Mrs. Benjamin. "You won't regret it."

Why would he regret eating a shrimp or two, a pear slice or two? She's condemning his skinniness.

"Leave him alone. The worst thing you can do to a teenager is watch him grow."

Who said this? Probably the woman who's talking to Connie, nodding her silvery head. Joan? Mrs. Seymour? Brian can't remember her name. He's not the sort of young man who would interrupt a conversation to ask someone's name. Jane?

"My son's a walking catastrophe." Mrs. Seymour glances sideways at Brian, and something freezes, for one moment, the side of her face. "All I know is, he won't do anything desperate."

"You're so calm, Jane. How do you know? The teachers say Tony needs regular counseling."

"Educators!" Mrs. Seymour chokes, spits a fleck of ice across the table. The candle flame hisses and cracks. "Faith. That's how."

Mrs. Seymour's dinner companion shifts in his chair. He's over six feet tall and even quieter than Brian, more suited to silence.

Brian's thoughts are slippery maggots, his face a puzzle of movement. It's easier, he decides, to remember men's names. The man with Mrs. Seymour is Gary Hansen. He used to play baseball. Mrs. Seymour takes Gary's hand.

"Where is the bathroom?" Brenda is asking someone—where is the bathroom?

"Over there." Laura admits vaguely that she's not sure.

"I'll find it." Don't go! Brian thinks so loudly he's afraid he's said it.

Brenda disappears, following Mrs. Cherry, the wife of the restaurant proprietor.

Mrs. Benjamin flips her fingers as a silencing gesture at her husband.

"What, dear?" Mr. Benjamin talks loudly. Mrs. Benjamin leans forward, the angular shelf of her bosom pushing against her plate.

"Sss ... the ... supposed to ... sss ... matter ... us."

"I don't know, Martha. I'm sure if you asked them, they'd ... "

"What time is it?"

Brian tells Tom it is eight o'clock.

Tom is casting about for a new conversation. He considers Gary, the ex-athlete, then leans suddenly toward Brian.

"What did you say you do, Brian?"

Mrs. Seymour's neck lengthens and her eyes dart for plates.

"Oysters?" she says politely.

"Here, Jane," says Tom, reaching in front of Herbert Benjamin. Herbert's dinky dark eyes scrutinize his wife's tight lips. She's mouthing something again.

Brian clutches at linen under the table—the tablecloth scrapes like a skirt across his pants.

"So, what do you do?" Tom asks again. Tom asks questions to be asked questions.

"Encode firearms."

"Huh?"

"Serial numbers, key-punching."

"Where were we?" Mr. Benjamin twists in his chair to face Tom. His shoulder juts over the table, a glacial ridge. Jane abandons Connie and vies for a word with the men.

"Dad, Gary and I read that book, and what we think ... "

"Who's Gary?"

"I'm Gary."

"I'm terribly sorry, Gary."

Gary looks blank. Herbert looks certain.

"I met you last month at that cast party. You and Jane came with my grandson."

"I'm afraid not." Gary looks uneasily at Jane. Jane looks miserably at all of them.

Mrs. Benjamin uncorks a bottle of white wine. "Brian? Your glass is empty." Brian can't tell his glass from Brenda's. He lets her fill both of them. Where is Brenda?

Mr. Benjamin tells a story about losing his passport at the Cairo airport. "Laura was already on the plane. So was Brenda's and Brian's mother. The stewards were running around. 'Passport of Ben-ya-meen, Ben-ya-meen passport.' I'm not kidding. I thought it was over." Mrs. Benjamin twists her watchband. The men and women at the table are laughing.

"Mushrooms," says Mrs. Benjamin. "How's that sauce? This one's good. It reminds me of lemon, but I know it's not."

Brian stands. The edge of the tablecloth goes up with him, clings to his belt buckle, so he must beat it down. Everyone looks at him. The two old ones at the end glare at him coldly, four stupid eyes.

"Where's the bathroom?" Brian asks Mrs. Cherry.

"Down here." She leads the way.

"That's not for you," says Mrs. Cherry. "Yours is over here."

"What I want is ... "

"You can't go in there. See the dress. Yours has pants. What you want?"

"A girl. Dark hair? Is she in there?"

Mrs. Cherry sizes him up, his crumpled shirt, digital watch. She pushes against the door of the ladies' room. "What's the name?"

66

"Brenda."

Before the door shuts, Brian glimpses floral walls, rows of light bulbs reflected in a mirror, someone's swinging foot. He sits on a bench under the pay phone and rolls and unrolls his sleeves.

Herbert Benjamin's voice boxes its way down the hallway: "I'm not saying that people can't read the book, I'm saying it's … "

"What are you waiting for?" Brenda stands over him, her chin a little wet.

"Let's get out of here."

"We can't just leave."

"You did," he says.

"Maybe I feel sick. I'm trying to cope, at least."

"I don't like those people."

"Tell them you're an artist. They'll talk to you then."

"Artist?"

Brenda's eyelids thicken and shut. She's counting. "I'm—not—talking to you." She runs back into the ladies' room. Brian imagines tearing off Mrs. Cherry's dress, putting it on, flapping its black and white wings.

He goes to the men's room. One of the bulbs is burned out. It's cold. The walls are baby-blue tile. There isn't even a mirror. He spits in a urinal, tucks in his shirt.

"Brenda, how about you? Here's Brian. Brian, would you like some more?" Mrs. Benjamin is a huge monarch butterfly. She puts turkey and a dab of cranberry on a little painted plate and pushes the plate at Brian. She feeds everyone.

"I'm fine. Thanks, Mrs. Benjamin." He has killed himself in the bathroom. His mind is empty.

"Brenda, some of this?"

"No, really, we're fine."

Mrs. Benjamin shrugs and scrapes the rest of the spinach and all except one carrot onto her plate.

Under the table Brian takes Brenda's hand. Brenda sips from her teacup, but it's empty.

"They're all out of sherbet. How disappointing."

"I'm full, anyway."

"Look at you two. Who would think you're brother and sister, the way you get along."

Mrs. Seymour cocks her head from one side to the other. An ice cube slides between her molars and bulges at the side of her jaw.

"Herbert, a toast?"

"Let's finish this damned wine."

"To health"

"And good reviews."

All the people raise their glasses, clink them and sip. "Not a late night for me."

"We'll take all three cars."

"Suppose you borrowed one, just for the night?"

"It broke. I couldn't believe it, but it did. It just ... broke." Brian moves his arm, and the talking resumes.

"Tomorrow I go."

"All the expectations in the world."

"I've tried, he's still not home."

"Tomorrow then."

"Shall we?"

"Let's."

"Is this anyone's scarf?"

Brenda takes her scarf and plays for a moment with the fringe. Brian lifts her coat from the back of her chair and helps her into it. He touches her sleeve, but she doesn't feel it. Everyone is standing. Everyone faces in a slightly different direction.

The group moves slowly toward the door, buttoning, talking, digging for keys.

"Follow me in the black one."

"It's cold out there. Zip up!"

Brenda runs ahead of Brian. She catches up to Laura. She says something.

Basal Distance

if it didn t have periods and commas it d be a poem about apostrophes and question marks about scenery do you have scenery a winter ride to the lebanese psychiatrist the reason to go to the psychiatrist is so men and women won t have to but tell them about it later so they can benefit from it i said my anxiety on tuesdays is revolting it used to be workshop day i used to like LIKE workshop day but ten years without workshop comma tuesdays eat me what is causing your reaction he asked war i said he said are you like the rest of us and you disagree with war yes i said i disagree with war and he said only one man agrees with war but he won t go to the war then he told me try meditation and i said it s not enough you must have a teacher for meditation on tuesdays an elevator is going up and down inside my body s frame not quote unquote mental an elevator is going up and down inside my body s frame not italics mental italics basal dash basal than mental double dash basal distress better than quote unquote mental illness in reject that label we experience it for them or driving in a winter glass to the doctor at eight early tend the gist you are seeking and save them red tape paperwork and general satisfaction of given treatment call it basal distance or basal distress not mental illness i heard the african american woman psychologist say her wards are mentally sick are white sick ones her black patients hurts typical i said raising my hand basal distance question mark might it be long before mental illness basal distance fills it next question mark

Laidlaw

There were too many laws but not enough of the kinds she wanted. She wished for the right to go shopping. Then taste rather than disposable income or access to finance could distinguish people. The right to create appealed to her, as did the rights to be paid to work and paid to be. Those rights extended to some but not all married people. There were intelligible people without desirable rights and unintelligible people with desirable rights. Desirable as compared to rote rights were privileges. Laidlaw was a surname and a bus company. As slang it delivered desirable duty. One could press someone to service in an economy where comparable worth carried no legal value. One could press someone to service in the name of status or prestige. Services that carried a fee such as dry cleaning, with its long counter that separated customers from dry cleaning staff, struck people as necessarily costly rather than necessarily free. Proficiency in one's native language seemed free like water or air, though water itself was not free and air was difficult to regulate. Laws she cared little for were Canadian. In Canada, aspirin with codeine in it was available without prescription, yet someone in America, who had drunk one drink over the legal limit twenty years in the past could be barred admittance to Canada as a tourist or worker or visiting relative. A Canadian resident told her that Canadians in small towns drank and drove through the mountains. The resident's husband had been convicted of a felony in a tavern fight. He was permitted to cross either border. Sometimes the law punished someone when something bad might have happened. That was a type of law she didn't understand. In jails were people who had harmed no one but whose chance of hurting someone unintentionally had increased by a given behavior on a given occasion. That they might have hurt someone yet did not seemed inadequate justification to incarcerate them. It seemed cause for celebration!

Next Time, Academics

Culinary topics. My beautiful message got lost when the screen jumped. I'll retype it from memory, but it will be a rewrite. Food 48 hours in jail in 2003 for one beer over the legal limit (high beam out one-quarter mile), one topic, women in jail, other topic, why women are in jail, other topic, food in Illinois, where I stopped overnight, on the way back from Savannah by car, another topic, and beer, last topic. Here was the gist: I should have ordered the chicken at the truck stop diner, since I already knew going by the soup, that the food at the truck stop was as bad as the food in jail (barbed-wire medium security in Plymouth, Minnesota), the worst food I've ever tasted despite the chicken and biscuits on that M.L.K., Jr. holiday, my check-in day. The spareribs I ordered after a fifteen-hour drive were boiled and looked hoary. The diner did not sell beer, but there was a flesh shack down the road and the advertised largest cross in the world; in fact, there are flesh shacks, adult superstores, ADULT on a road sign, throughout Illinois and even in Wisconsin, where at least the citizenry (employees at the food-and-gas store) are politically well-versed and did not see their taxes go to public Bible schools, as in Illinois. I suggested after we passed the flesh shack, that we turn around, and that I go in and say to the sex workers that the Russians are fetching $3.5 K per hour in Manhattan and it's private, unlike there at that road-side shack. Plus, the clients, if they are inclined, and they like a gal, whatever her age, may pick up the $1.75 K-per-hour tax tab. How about that? I wouldn't know what a corn-fed without a European accent might fetch without mob ties, but maybe it would be better than pole dancing by the Illinois freeway. My travel companion, though he smiled wryly at my speech, did not wish to co-liberate sex workers that late at night. Who delivers Peroni in Minneapolis on Sunday? Imagine WOMAN on a road sign.

Écriture de la chatte

Another writer was not always another writer. Before that she was a young woman writer and before that a girl who wrote, before that a child and before that an infant, before that an egg in the scenic camaraderie of heaven, in a film about two pants, parents enjoining her to take up.

She has lived with her and inside her. Has she seen it? She has not seen it, but she has roamed its hall until airborne, a cord dripping. Who cut it? Saw. He saw it, the boy, from the foot of his mother's death bed, her covers flung off—dark furry snail suddenly visible—signal of what's next, his dying at the beginning or her end.

Another writer writes a serious paw, a mistake of cat, a dripping maw, a dune of replacement. "Sex is a renewable resource," she says. "If I have slept with all of North America, then you have slept with all of North America and Iceland besides. Wake up, lizard!" but he has slid off the bed.

She'd rather write his penis than her pussy. She's seen *that*.

Her clit is off limits to all except a stranger. He sends her a chestnut-sized, hand- painted black and pink-petaled vibrator with twelve speeds and two gyrations. When it runs out of energy, she plugs in the long one, long like a rolling pin.

"It was the size of my forearm," she said when he asked her about the largest man. "I squatted over it. The head was inside me, and I covered only the top of it like a helmet. He didn't thrust."

She is long and curved up near a bell; only the carillonneur has knocked it.

She goes to the garden in August with her camera. She pictures it for the wild rhinoceros, a serious writer, living in Reading. She has never met him. He sends her fifty photos of his pumped-up self, even one of his erection during a handstand. She says, "I'm not big enough for you, not wide." He texts her from a restaurant in Philly where he is eating mussels: *when r u cum-ing?*

In the photo an elegant nail partitions the leaves: a flower, she's heard that, or an ear of prime rib. She posts the photo to her weblog under the heading "Sex and Taxes" and leaves it for fowl to peck at for a week.

"I don't want you to get a Brazilian," he tells her, only he calls it a Bolivian. She has to get a Brazilian, every few weeks for a year. "I like you with hair there," he says, "I like women with hair there," but his position is a losing climb. "Suit yourself," he says, "but it's for men who fantasize girls." "It's cleaner," she says, thinking of the artist in St. Paul who wouldn't let hair near his mouth. She has told him about the camera but not about the rhinoceros who texts her in Reading: gitting any? like a common pornographer or a crowd.

Blood everywhere, and this time she hasn't prepared for him or shaved. Fifteen pillow shams at the Palmer House devastated, a serious poet from Philadelphia, not the writer from Reading after all.

The third first he: Had he seen it? The ring. He couldn't move forward to be inside it with her: It was a deadlock in several positions. He went down to look at her, to shell gaze. There was a wedding band. "You said you weren't a virgin when I met you," he said. "I'm not," she said. And he turned it.

Almanac

Marcy called on the abortion day. She had been reading from Source Almanac.

"Wisconsin produces more beer and brandy than any place, and furthermore, Milwaukee is a better city than Minneapolis, in all areas except one thing ... "

"The police force," I said. "Milwaukee police beat people like Philadelphia police beat people and bomb people."

"And of the ten cities with most bars per capita, Wisconsin has six of them."

Then I knew that four years at college, beer with Marcy and everyone we met may not have been normal. It had been a way to meet lonely people who were secretly brilliant and unfit to live how they must in this place.

I said, "Marcy, Source Almanac is a guide for the Apple."

In Moscow there are oxygen tanks on the street because everyone drinks too much, like here, like Wisconsin. Maybe the students can't move from within.

I thought then of Robert, who was brilliant and spoke pure poetry, how we met the only time in a bar and I loved him. He said, "Kill or be killed," and he yelled at me because I couldn't shoot a gun.

I said, "Robert, I thought you were in mathematics."

And he said, "Turnip, you little nothing sassy, kill or be killed."

Then the other guys, who had been to Vietnam, too, said, "Robert, sit down."

The Gift

That's it. The rest is history. And history is never as interesting as what your imagination can give you. History is what you get when the projector gets stuck.

It turns out that art, like everything else, is what some people do for a living. Art, what passes for it, is a commodity. It is just one more thing to pay for, lug home with you, borrow, or steal—hurtar para dar por Dios, as it says in the dictionary.

If I could rouse any interest, I would start a support group for people committed to art. I would circulate a petition, start an internal movement to bust people out of the art hospital. I would get a witness to say that I were healthy enough to live on my own, to make a decent living. What is stopping me is thinking that I am bound to the commitment I made to art as a child.

One way to make something real is in solitary confinement. Some people walk with God and honor their commitments. Those people may live anywhere on Earth except in the limelight.

Lock-up, I queried. Where is lock-up?

I would not have asked where lock-up is had I known it would seem forensic.

The first thing you find out in lock-up is that God exists. In other situations you could just dismiss this information. In lock-up that is impossible. The second thing you find out is that God is everywhere, even in you. Your job as an artist is to come up with a reasonable gift to present to God.

Most people who go into the art hospital never get out. They just get moved to more comfortable quarters. Some of them, the invalids and life-long convalescents, live on the deluxe wing. The worst thing is knowing that deep down I want to stay. I would show no sign of resistance if they offered me a room with a view. "Put the trophies over there," I would tell my students from my comfortable bed.

For about one month out of solitary I would have appreciators. There would be no question about it—I had served both God and man. After that, if I managed to do anything more, they would give me students. It is very strange, these students. They come from miles around to be put in the hospital with you. Most of them are starving and craven. Usually it is because they had a parent or step-parent who belonged in one hospital or another themselves but who managed to hold on by sheer will power to the world outside. Then values changed, and these offspring lost the wherewithal to define their own existence. There are millions and millions of them, and their numbers are growing. There never will be enough beds.

The easiest wholesale solution is for everyone to drink their gift to death. That way is the most popular, but it is not the only possibility.

If people were willing to open their minds a bit, they could find constructive uses for creative energy. They could leave the hospital, even for day trips, and no one would blame them for changing their minds. They could write to their congressmen. They could volunteer at shelters for the homeless; better yet, they could go on the road with Jimmy Carter and build habitats for humanity. They could sing in the church choir. They could grow a garden. They could raise their own children. We do not need as much art as we are making. There are many other things we need more.

Some people, women especially, go the sex route. They devote their ingenuity to making themselves as sexy as movie stars. Artists can never be worshipped as mindlessly as movie stars, but some of them come pretty close. Other artists, the men especially, sleep around or mulch up their brains on fame.

The very lucky few get shipped back to solitary confinement. Most of these do not know they are lucky, chosen. They think they are being punished for bad reviews. They think bad reviews cheat. They think good reviews tell the truth.

There is no need to worry about art. Art in its ideal forms stays safe. Real art resists being the object of attention. It directs your gaze, and it swings in you forever.

Of the inmates with windows, every year, one or two of them, the purest at heart, beg to be let back into the cell. They are afraid they will jump. That would be going beyond the call of duty, something no one might say. They say that they have learned their lesson, and they promise all the real powers-that-be that they will work harder this time. They sign statements to that effect and they apologize to their loved ones for the emotional and financial turmoil they have caused and will continue to cause until death. (In some of them, the very exemplary, this bad behavior will be held up as customary, even as tax-exempt.) They say goodbye to them and vow never to look outside themselves for companionship or diversion again. Of course, it does not last. Pretty soon someone or something better comes along.

They all have one thing in common. They discovered their gift in the first place because they needed a friend, so they made one up. They kept on making things up until they had a world. Now that they have real friends, and sex, you would think they could just let it rest, but they can't. They still have something to prove, so they put their name on the waiting list to perform their very own, original talent shows in the seasick cafeteria.

Most of the shows are the same, except in detail. It is rare indeed when someone gets the wind whipping through your grapevine. These days most anything is acceptable as an offering—a stick of wood, a drum roll, a shitty conversation ya had with a friend. The ones who feel ashamed of their limitations almost quit.

It was better in the days before promotion, when having a gift meant something in Latin. In God, a token to His allness in your smallness. A simple nest egg.

First Appearances

Dumb Luck — *Argotist Ebooks*, 2010

Credenza, Big English, Un Americano, Irish Salad, Two Hundred Fifty, Dreams-in-progress, Basal Distance, Écriture de la chatte — *Argotist Ebooks*, 2011

Hors d'oeuvre, Chinese — The Quarterly

Primary Creative — *Big Bridge*

Almanac, Hogging the Lady — *Poetic Inhalation*

The Gift, Next Time, Academics — *Mad Hatters' Review*

Thrice Words With Ann Bogle

How did you find your particular voice, as a writer? Where did this sound, these connections you make that give the work a reading apart and separate, come from?

I think I was born with a voice. I've read a paper I wrote in sixth grade that my mother typed. I can hear or see my voice in that paper. It's an exploration of the six wives of Henry VIII. I sought the topic because I wanted to study lives of famous women. When I was older and enrolled in writing workshops, there was talk of finding one's writer voice, and I assumed I was just starting out and did not yet have a writer's voice. But now I can see that I had one all along. The voice is like a thumbprint or sense of individuality. I employ different stylistic techniques and attitudes. I write in different lengths. I think voice remains evident whether the approach is linear or poetic.

It's quite distinctive. Have you ever attempted to maintain it over the course of long form material? Most of your work is in the flash or short story form. Are there any novels in there? Past, present, or future?

I have one novella, and the voice is there. The length is 120 pages. I also have written a 300-page journey of the self. The voice is there. The 300-page work covers the dimensions of religion, diary, memoir, and fantasy. I am writing a memoir now. I have no definite plan to write a novel.

Do you have a regular process, a schedule or a time to spend writing, or does it happen when it happens of its own accord?

When I am writing something book length, I write daily in the afternoon, and I aim for 500 words. There were times in the past when I wrote daily without limit. I once wrote 14 single-spaced pages in one day. This time, with the memoir, I'm writing a typed page and a half each day. I try to draft with pen or pencil, but I can never stick to it. I give up on handwriting, though I know from experience that longhand improves quality. That's a conflict that I find hard to resolve. Typing I often revise as I go, so there is no first draft. That is especially true with my page-long pieces. I rewrite an uncountable number of times. With page-long pieces I write when the mood strikes rather than for an hour or two in the afternoon. One of my pieces that later won recognition from Wigleaf ran 147 words and took sixteen hours of continuous effort.

Do you fit yourself into any kind of a "school," or genre? Do you consider what you do realism, or absurdist , or do any of those labels matter to you at all? There doesn't seem to be an immediately classifiable place to put you. I don't understand the need for people to do that but be that as it may, if you were to do it, where to you classify or most closely classify your work as?

In my short stories, there is often a linear timeline, and the substance is fiction. In memoir pieces there is often circular reasoning, and the factual basis is often blurred or concealed by my pose when I create. I am a graduate of three creative writing programs — U.W.-Madison, Binghamton University, and U of Houston — and I practice fidelity to all I learned there and that I was there. Not every graduate values their creative writing program experience, but I do. I think as graduates we were susceptible to influence by our peers and teachers. I see it as an inheritance of experience. So while a label may not stick to that, there is an imprint. In my case, I was urged to stay with my instincts and not to fight against them.

Along those lines, then, who do you read? Not who you merely admire or who is influential. But who do you read?

I recently read a few memoirs written by people I don't know and people I do. I picked up a biography of Donald Barthelme, along with a series of his fiction books, short stories mainly. I read a recent book of stories by Padgett Powell. I read a novel by Larry Woiwode and two of his nonfiction books. These were teachers of mine except for Barthelme, who was my teacher's teacher. A writer new to me is Chavisa Woods, whose memoir of sexism is called 100 Times.

On the subject of what a writer reads, probably the most common bromide you'll hear is something along the lines of "if you want to learn how to write the best thing to do is to read, read, read." Yet some say if they read too much they start to see other writer's style pop up in their own work. You have any thoughts on that?

That kind of imprinting actually furthers one's own voice and vision. One thinks one may sound like another more famous author, but in fact one still sounds like oneself. True, an attitude of the other author may creep in, and the style of the writing may seem unlike other pieces one has written.

You don't talk like you write. How do you get in that zone?

I'm convinced it's attitude, and I mean that in an artistic not a social sense. I think I literally hold my shoulders in a different position as if I'm going in for football and then I launch my pea shooter, and I have to fire many rounds at the page. My writing in the memoir is linear and direct, and it seems vaguely inartistic, but it serves my purpose for it now.

I'm surprised to hear that because so much of what we're presenting here "sounds" like memoir, or at least first person expose. Now, maybe it's fiction here, but - out of curiosity - why the change?

I don't understand the question. My understanding of interview is to answer in the first person and relate the answers to life or in our case to writing. I switched to metaphor to describe how I position myself for writing creatively.

Maybe it's me. I got the impression the memoir you are working on was being done without the kind of literary approach that makes the Ann Bogle voice the Ann Bogle voice. You have a grand ability to turn not only a phrase but an expected

metaphor on its head—in my opinion. That's what makes you, *you*. I somehow got the impression you were going straight for the memoir you are working on. I could have misinterpreted.

I have a strong interest in linear narration for the book-length memoir and that curtails much of the play I usually enlist, but there is still turn of phrase. It's still me but simplified. I realized that certain writers on Facebook and Fictionaut were saying that my short pieces were too baffling. I don't regret writing them, but I needed to regroup and think of longer projects that gave me a sense of clarity.

Exactly the opposite of what I would suggest, if asked. Exactly the opposite. But you know you better than I do.

The writing goal is clarity in the memoir. I am writing it with an audience in mind and would love to see it published by a publisher. I would love to find an agent to represent it. I would hesitate to self-publish it because I have heard that route is actually hard. A publisher once told me that memoirs only have a chance if the author is famous or has killed someone. Neither is true here. I'm not holding my breath but one can hope.

Thank you, Ann.

Ann Bogle

Born in St. Louis Park, Minnesota
Hometown Minnetonka, Minnesota
Place of residence now: St. Louis Park, Minnesota
Educated in Hopkins schools, Minnesota
University of Wisconsin-Madison, B.A. English major
Binghamton University, M.A. fiction writing & English
University of Houston, M.F.A. fiction writing & English

Ann Bogle's works of short fiction and prose poetry have appeared in *Asymptote, New World Writing, Wigleaf, Big Bridge, Thrice Fiction, Wordgathering,* and forty-five other publications. Her work has been anthologized in *The Right Way to be Crippled* and *Naked* (Cinco Puntos Press) and other volumes. Her chapbooks were published by Dusie Press, Argotist, and Xexoxial Editions. Her reviews were published in *Fictionaut, American Book Review,* and *Rain Taxi.* Interviews appeared in *Fictionaut* and other places. She lives in St. Louis Park, Minnesota near where she was born.

Photo by David Sherman Photography

The Anaphora House
by Amantine Brodeur

Prologue

She stood in the doorway and watched Gavin lace his black boots with white shoelaces. Sylvie was staring at the bristling of her brother's recently shaven head, across the top sheen of his skull when the words spilled into the space between them;

- Do you collect god or swastikas?

- What do you know about it? He snapped back, lifting his head to scowl at her from under his dark eyebrows.

He reminded her of a snarling dog. She tried to imagine his lips unfurl and his teeth gripped in a foamy growl. She stared at him for a few seconds before running down the corridor and slamming her bedroom door. She lay curled up on the bed, fighting the tears, mystified at the stranger her brother was becoming, as if drawing breath and his inner life out of the thick gore of graphic novels, scarce and loud — the makings of an immense threat.

She heard him say her name. She drew herself up out from under cover and sat up.

Now, he was leaning against her bedroom doorframe. His dark gothic style making him unbearingly handsome.

- All I know is you're turning into an immense bully. I saw you the other day.

- Where?

She stood up, leaving the bedcover rumpled. She drew a deep breath. She stood still, feeling her insides withering from his 20 seconds' stare.

- What did he ever do to you? Her hands squeezing grief that would stain for life.

- That's not the point.

- What is it then? Explain it to me!

The Blue Cypress

In this city of thunder, children are made from what the thunder said; voices mud-raked, silent and dead. Expression of utterly cold skin. Apropos of nothing; deliberate voices of undressing without having to breathe a word in the din. Our construction begins in the small dressing room lined with lights; where personas find breath and bones, costumed to their lines and pinned to the stage of stones. We dance among the tombstones and mock the men in black frocks. Each gave on less than the other, each day the stakes moved beyond: And there centre-stage, setting the baseline of it all, the thin tall man, borrowing his shadow from ghosts.

At the moment of being named, is the thing invented or made visible? Subjectivity of raw research. The imagination of naming a thing that had nothing to do with its own principle of existence beforehand. Limitations of gathering collections. Pinning insects to a board: mounting nature in death making it demonstrable – value of creating familiar things. How did the world see itself at a time when a tree or a cloud had no name? What then is love without its naming ? Love – Passion, a guiding hand to suicide, *Laquearia* Virgil's Aeneid. Dido – Queen of Carthage her passion for Aeneid leads to her suicide, Cleopatra's love of Anthony commits suicide. Plath … Hughes. A line on a grey scale from light to white to the deep unforgiven black. Colossal and tender bravado. Capricious and intimate. The pose. Sophistication of all that fake desire; the haunting poise of skin, in its haecceity, silent in astonished eroticism. Exploring the instability of proximity – in the elasticity of its shadows: I am not the tongue made of marrow or from fibres spun out of shadows. The poet waits for me in the doorway. Reluctant me lingers at a distance, and oh so bloody petulant, in a mood brimming with venom and reticence. As if taking steps towards myself are those of surrender. Seeking to make ground in the chase after time as perpetual memory. Seeking to make ground in the chase after time as perpetual territory. Which childhood run amuck? Finding roots of words. Words of / in roots. Rooted wording. The word finds its roots. It's all Taxonomy. Type-written Midnight; real or imagined? Over-ripe. Intellect preening like a dead crow. The air is wet and dark with black ink. His version of tender; me, a mangy dog made to follow a roadside life, loathsome, racking in its wakeful dying.

Sylvie stood quite still, nausea rising, imperceptibly at first; Gavin's voice had darkened and slowed. He was seated on the floor behind a pane of glass. She had no way to reach him. Ward guards stood behind her. There were three others inside the glass frame. Gavin spun round, still seated on the floor. He was talking to someone. She knew who it might be:

" . . . .to the hunch of recently bought books she began the untidy activity of reading; her mind fidgeting like a restless child, a chewing stare through the scattered ink; those Executive styled fonts soaked as if drunk on Sassicaia from the Tyrrhenian coast – moaning the black and white aren't woven into truffle pages – such a waste of edible words . . ."
His voice trailed off. His gestures stopped. Sylvie knew he recognized that she had entered the room. He sat unmoving for some time.

- Your invisible friend; Mr. Cognito: He tells you to ask the right
    questions: Why do I have knees rather than fins, eyes, not
    feelers¿ Why am I me and not a cat or a bird or a flower, or
    rain ¿
He crawled toward the glass. Sylvie anticipated his looking up at her, or his standing; he did neither. He raised his palm and spoke to it.
    - Am I transparent or nature's indifference¿
She wanted to kneel, but he was already shuffling across the floor back to the pile of rubble.
Sylvie felt faint, her hands began shaking. She held herself and breathed deeply. the Staff Nurse reached out to assist her. Sylvie brushed her hand away.
    - What is it he's doing *this* time ¿

The elderly woman smiled and replied; " Empires of Toast."

Empires of Toast

Blinders. Instinctive language.
Eating made easy.
Anti-inflammatory adventures.

Favours.
Silence.
Never argue with a dead person.
Past is a different country – REMEMBER !!!!
Winsome skimming.
Ventriloquist
able to confess
his own true voice.   Authentic stuff.
Book-length thoughts.
Figuring poetry of itself.
Glimpse of idioms coining a turn of phrase.
Peroxide literariness.   For the otherwise tender squeeze of
easy cliché.
A notch or two. The hollow crisp gardener of lost and found:
Purposeful temperance of war and memorabilia.
To collect the awkward affections never noticed.
Vulnerable
against
the
bleak
vinyl backseat. Bubble wrap pops
balloons explode
sending the dog, tail-tucked, under the table into the narrow
sensuous rhetoric of lovelorn fear.

Mopping up the loose ends of living blurred
miles of mundane hours.
Rural
fittings of sheep's wool
and upturned palms of fields.

At the banquet of ignorance. Ranunculus.
At the level of a sentence. The failure to be dangerous.

What is there to remember?
Frail volumes
of lives fastened
on one side. The crisp anguish
of a random
act of life. A garland
oflightbetweenleaves.

Prosody.
Why does the end   of the
spinelooklikeaphallus?
How deep can a man be at his height?

A
badly
bruised copy . . .?
Opening truths
to
softer
selves.

If one could hammer-in history; pin time's tail
                    to the wall and call it a donkey;
play spin the bottle and hangman, roping every
                    thing into a big dark heart of indelible ink
and feed it morsels of immortality in a poetic
                    Afterlife.
Accumulated images shoved like a shunt as if to relieve some pres-
sure on the proviso life stitched its sparrow spine wishful sinking of
flight. It had been a forgotten memory; the details of it. The surge
of forgetfulness, that urge to say the same old things, rote by dismal
rote. And all for that instantaneous shame. It never really left her. She
watched him through the glass knowing this would be the last time:

His canvas plantations of blue cypress trees standing vivid against the chipped, dirty yellow walls. The large mirror he'd once demanded stood vacated; all the smashed shards long gathered up 'in the interests of safety'.

The state of humour as he pages through catalogue proofs munching his light ham brioche. Monied masculine muscle. Reaching for the porcelain handle of the milk jug to pour into coffee. *He doesn't like it black.*

The rectangles of colour and form – same abstracted features – wonder at the millions he assesses in the flip of the pages. Paper yellow folder; the muscle of art business. The dwindling of archaic smells as the building atrophies beyond neglect into decaying irrelevance.

She stole his laces. How could she have forgotten ?

Thoughts stretch like old nylon, yet it only pulls so far before a running tear slits an eye in half. That width of love. And punctual obedience. Pejorative deployment. An act of pure clarity. Insensate coruscation Unreachable blank … distress, the distance of bellies: Just a boy pulling his heart out in the alley behind the Gents. Always at the edge pf privilege: Its weft and weave, a cut, a slice, a stitch beyond her.

Rhododendron circles And all that discretion, that discreet light of plush company, embedded in the dark of elegant desires. Deep mires of cautious talk while Memo Belles dance the isles among the tall edges of small minds. Unpleasant avenues uncommon paths - Always a ministry of misery: The crawl of bare-chested men; mornings in the feel of improvisation to the appearance of memory.
Recalcitrance of a concrete skyline reaching upward as if mimicking expressionless bookends, bidding goodnight to the city. Loss of distinctive scale. The parody of small catastrophes.

"Are you alright Miss?" The policewoman's voice repeated several time before Sylvie felt herself resurface back into the present.
"Sorry, what …?"

Sylvie tried to orientate to the noise and bustle of people, the bright lights, the cordon tape hissing as it was unraveled around the crime scene.

Squinting and holding her hand up against the light, she saw her hand covered in blood. Her gasp drew heads from other police officers, some reflex-reaching for their holsters. Sylvie vaguely registered the policewoman gesturing with her hands to those strangers to do nothing. Sylvie writhed as she tried to stand, collapsing into the grasp of the paramedic who stood aside her, explaining the state in which he'd found the two of them, when he'd arrived from the emergency call.
Sylvie felt her body wretch and the tears flow uncontrollably. Clarity hit, hit back hard, and she realized, she had just murdered her brother.

Sylvie's Tea Pavilion

A breakfast of conundrums; that puzzling helix of breath
　　　　　and kisses gathered to cheek bones. Naked warnings.

　　　Incandescent neon when the Idea of itself collapses and the
pile of bones shipped off to the laundry, return, scrubbed dry and
　　　　　　　　　　　　　　　　　　　　reticent.

　　　Between foul and water, where do birds come into play?
　　　　　Songs composed on herringbone tongues.

The hollow space of curious ideas unable to hold their own.

　　　Wingbone of a sparrow caught in the lies of love, particulates
　　　　　　　　　　　　　　　　　　of error.
　　　　　　　Or would that be Terror?

Classification. Naming. Order. Systems indicative of natural relationships. Evolutionary. Taxis -method. Taxa – hierarchical groups hierarchy of values. Study of living organisms. Systematic classification.

Cladistic analysis. System of biological taxonomy. Quantative analysis of comparative data. Cladograms.

Assessing evolutionary history. Proposal. Educative objective.

Provocative transactions
Dubious stuff.
To stare down the static consequences of beauty
She eats freshly hot cookies of dark chocolate as if the dark
invisible melt under her tongue, she might escape herself for good.

Spring to the dark race as if mud could provide some deadline
Baroque delta
Tireless gait
Give me the still mending of the world.

Slick of the Young for whom smudge is some foreign rhetoric
of our age, far beyond their country of origin.

She stood in the doorway and watched Gavin lace his black boots with white shoelaces. Sylvie was staring at the bristling of her brother's recently shaven head, across the top sheen of his skull when the words spilled into the space between them;
"Do you collect god or swastikas?"

"What do you know about it?" He snapped back, lifting his head to scowl at her from under his dark eyebrows.
He reminded her of a snarling dog. She tried to imagine his lips unfurl and his teeth gripped in a foamy growl. She stared at him for a few seconds before running down the corridor and slamming her bedroom door.

She lay curled up on the bed, fighting the tears, mystified at the stranger her brother was becoming. Drawing on the thick gore of graphic novels, scarce and loud – the makings of an immense threat.
"All I know is you're turning into an immense bully. I saw you the other day."

"Where?"
She stood up, leaving the bedcover rumpled. She drew a deep breath
She stood still, feeling her insides withering over at the 20 seconds stare.
"What did he ever do to you?" Her hands squeezing grief that would
stain for life.
"That's not the point!" Gavin was pissed off now.
"What is it then, explain it to me?" . . .

> Waking to clouds in ordinary light;
> how to be drawn or eaten. *The Done Thing*
> is dead and buried.

> Arms crossed life, folded
> across the chest as if wrapped
> against the Dangerous.
> In the quadrant of orange paint: theft.
> Frozen embryo.
> Memory or salt?
> Herringbone fingers.

> Crisp brittle affection and
> cigarette burns around the ankle.

> The air of regret
> breathes in denial and watching
> Iggy Pop's girlfriend being devoured by a TV screen,
> reminisces about spurious romanticism

> of life
> as performance,

> rather than it embodying
> thinking without drugs.

Crawling out of a series
of survivals; love as a requiem for laughter . . .

Epilogue

White cloths and porcelain generosity.
God's breath – a line of rust blackening an immaculate opus. Dropping sins, peeling
sticky guilt off backbones in those quiet cells of urgent confession.
Plates of ash. The smallest sea. Little turf of soul.

Liturgy, employer of lungs dispensing shareholding in grief.
The noise of greed. Bare back confessions.
God bleeds under the weight of knees pressed into the polished wood.
Rung below bowed heads to folded hands
- explicit bowls of sins
pickpocketing memory.
Small- town sinners hunting down benedictions; well-heeled prayers, shuffling hymns
– keeping score offline.

Harrowing pity. Groping for light. In the frail swell of neutral distance, hours carry vague evidence, shuffling hymns. A random blend of loneliness. Forgiveness shaken loose, like pocket change, for the cut-price sermon. Twist of fate.

Neglect quickens.

Sylvie sat handcuffed, at the back, *dressed in Black*,
the one colour Gavin disliked, on her.

In The Scattering of Tongues
by Amantine Brodeur

Beckettian Women, In Four Acts

ACT ONE. *Threshold of White*
ACT TWO *The Floorwalkers of Balal*
ACT THREE *Never – utterance Words*
ACT FOUR *The Quickening Body of Everything*

22 December 2019, on the occasion of
Samuel Beckett's untwining, 22 December 1989

ACT ONE. *Threshold of White*

Famished and forgetful, singing songs of the dead, this rendering; mournful reversal in the death of invisible things, of body offerings sage and lime, salted at the rim. These are our sniper tales; reimagined spells untwining voodoo, like ancient herbalists reading the old forest floor. I read your sunburnt prose of sage and wishbones of bird flight across Sumaria by fowls having to crawl for wings glued together. There is nothing to mourn there; to herethere still in the fleeing, and in departures of staying. Heartbeats crack the ceiling of the sky suddenly the rain has a fear of falling, there's a colour of dusk that falls at the curfew of love, amber in its distillation of taste and desire for immortality. Reckless notation emptying us of our usual recognisable objects. In the pavilion of beauty, we throng to the celebration of our gaze, playtime stories a sparse game in the witch hunts of kiss 'n tell. This hold of white has no rules of engagement, none of that surgical precision of satire to lose one's body in morse code possibility of its illusion, of such a thing as its future. Blindly ground by such flaws of scavengers in the de-boning of poems served in burnt fig leaves, we leave seeds displaced into countries, experts in desalination and waste; flowers paralysed by all that erroneous smoke. Scraping thorns from the insides of cheekbones blood dreams open to anything but rapture in the monotony of joy, pickled hearts in saran wrap lovage, the seasoning of foreign fish in their mysterious hush. In the paucity but not for long, your bluer scarce stare before them deep, namely the fullness of the great and its unchanging calm blooms deepest meaning, deeplove of mournful blasphemy, wide eyes unfelt forever waiting to take hold. Librettist of bodies

ACT TWO *The Floorwalkers of Balal*

Insentient Her. The shrill pace of nerve-endings withstanding the paring back of her body past mouths and through red and black moving scapes of fraught breath, following in footfalls, lipped texts rewriting its premiere. Suddenly they're there, fire lit wordings prescriptive directives leaving it as a question, down, in the dirt with the rest of us, and with all the problems of make up. Suddenly they're there. You phase them out, confessions of her last last theatre, work of uglier confessions in progress, uglier work in progress. At one point He suddenly fades up; should he fade up when or there, the actual characters costumed in text; all bare bones voice out this past, dissatisfied? Voices out of this past of Here, manufactured. Intellects keep falling, sounds from your unseen death mask. She is passing, immersive; say something. Time appears saying nothing. Too alone, many of the later ones fade up too fast, the present no longer with its journey; every conversation comes with baggage of wicked humour, engrossed irrational regions. Say something. Time arrives with nothing to declare. A pilgrim dropped down from the stars takes a seating by the tree insinuating the wrongful weighting of comedic lows of ankle-height. Coat-hangers, insentient, subversive and irresolute make a tree of so little money to play with, contemplating the pilgrim, seated in such paring back, it reminds him again of Her; insentient, Self through the dark, reaching, with-standing rays dulled, not exactly casting doubt on feeling, but feelingless-ness of the Moon, so in and out, not of herself, sitting moonfed, of herself subversive, or immersively knelt beside, dying clouds. Seatings by the tree, waiting, so little to play with, not coat hangers or trees but hung, hooked, looking for the switch, OFF. Immersive, engrossed, say SOMETHING: I not and go on to learn and unlearn, fraughtfully falling. Insentient, if not exactly, at least then, the breath finally seated, free of head strapped shoulders bound to buckling. Not just a physical stripping; deprivation, spared love, elemental, distinctive cracks retrieving the feral i .

ACT THREE *Never – utterance Words*

In this history of dying mouths, which haven't spoken in a Decade, Him in her Death Scene. Never-utterance words, Thoughts that didn't want to know: Ideas clean-shaven of their Crises didn't want to go: A life that never looks the part. In these parables of Outcome, they'd talk of thorns in the Mythology of Being; rooted by tufts of Byssal threads along the flowing edge of thistle goose-marsh; palisade, sow-thistle and woundwort. Such uncommon consciousness in a paper cup, such common mooring, such: Still she breathes with rudimentary candour, with the raw-rush pulse of an unfinished universe; her stride bold, relentlessly natural; her poise impolite and her charm unpolished. Natter and gossip, like the firm hand of rust, like old seahags adrift, eyes stark with the glaze of a viewless stare, the agape of earth, like love, always the runner-up. Bawdy teeth sit ajar with the patience of Godot, never got up to leave or arrive; the bite of air hissing against the grain. In the proposition of iconography of light: All Rights Reserved. Emphatic, yet derivative: Nothing more but the Unseen and unseen, the Idea of thin logic. An uncouth Century licking sustained injury; no white Flag or epiphanies surrender, just shell fragments to commemorate an Under-age war harvesting the sky of its Blue. In this re-opening of dreams words rhyme amongst themselves in narrow doorways. Like goosefat to the whipped charm of rubber bullets, lives tossed on the heated tongues of skillets;

organs sizzle: Tongues compressing wit again, seeking asylum in bruised voices, of women. in full invention of invitation Unfolding skins of women-ness, leaving a little something of this wait, azure blown. sliding from micron darkness through its mute mouth into the beautiful grain of sky; blue screeches the colour of lungs, trembling ocellate whispering unnamed forgetting, stirring the still of the night air within her. Giddy and fresh-cut Memory. Lithe history sucked up deep and slow, back into Behind of those old teeth. Of any once-old Desire, wretched Mouthprints, en-point sets dryly up against her once, younger Fragrance. Restless hunger. One foot gravesides, bones lie in wait for the Middling women at old fair Grounds locked in on the accidental axis of humour and quick facts; walking the boards of that bare stage inessential questions in the vulgar prattle of this novella-child posing up that pastoral apprenticeship in an unremitting arousal of denouement; rogue memories skirting inexhaustible hemlines of her inchoate desire: a taut concern between the naked and *Her* dead.

ACT FOUR *The Quickening Body of Everything*

Red mouthed, fresh and lithe with the wilding look of the moorland gaze, Belacqua gathers up all the allurements of heather across the folds hiding Tarns laid low in terrain rough and unwieldy; all that birthing for a walking shadow: *Not a word, not a deed, not a thought, not a need, not a grief, not a joy, not a girl, not a boy, not a doubt, not a trust, not a scorn, not a lust:* All those inorganic moorings and ephemeral sex when there is nothing to be done with bones. She fades sharply upward into the shape of the 2 Solitudes – equidistant from *"Arse to knees, say bd, feet say at c, head on right cheek at a. Then arse to knees say again ac, but feet at b and head on left cheek at d. Then arse to knees say again bd, but feet at a and head on right cheek at c. So on other four possibilities when begin again"* – into the absences of Emma: "Arse to knees, say bd, feet say at c, head on right cheek at a. Then arse to knees say again ac, but feet at b and head on left cheek at d. Then arse to knees say again bd, but feet at a and head on right cheek at c. So on other four possibilities when begin again"

Imagine . . . Self through the dark, reaching. Self through the dark, wrought. Who now? When now? All eyes away. Crisply, bodies begin and end to part and parts of bodies meld like lycra, bodybound and boundless in recuperative argument in the glaze of love. Time disappears, saying nothing. The floorwalkers leave Balal, as they return, sounding their death masks through feral cheekbones; highground for frescoes and skulls casting their eyes across typographies of heat and light. Lit, baring such uncouth licking, hapless-giddy pilgrims foraging cellular fictions: Give her up! I confess my first feeling – were she to offer up violence – all my lousy life he was looking lousy, peeked telling me forever and over about worms, wormed into misfortune there and not then there; always returning where the floor never alters; inorganic viewpoint: there and not – trapped. His women weaving Byssal thread, yarning desires in words, made of words, others' words containing more caves and chamberpots, all spittlecoated from voices of the past; and then he got frightened and made a clean breast, but she wanted to have it out; razor in the vanity bag, just in case. Wretched mouthprints, all deep and so low, beckoning him out by the blubber mouth, jowls of insurrection, never knowing the question or if that was a when without, should ever "HasBeen" aged 6, asked about his birth, his mother to the end of it all, suddenly furious , replied, "Fuck off!"

The Babble-Ons

by Eckhard Gerdes

Did I ever tell you about the Babel-Ons? No? Well, they were a secret experimental fiction society whose calling it was to subvert language in order to achieve social change. Their argument was that language could take us back to the Tower of Babel, or it could take us on toward senility, when, like infants, we babble on. Or was that infantilism? I am not sure. But in any case, the Babel-Ons were very real, and in no time at all they discovered how much easier it was for them to destruct than to construct, so, of course, they chose the path most traveled and decided to be destructive.

Oh, you weren't asking about that? Well, I guess I'm not surprised. No one ever does.

The yellow fields are filled with misdemeanors none of us want to recall.

The call of weathervanes is tempered by the wind of the pains you feel in your knees.

When you were young, you never thought that your knees would ever cause you everlasting pain.

When you fell while roller skating, and your knee was split open wide with gravel embedded inside, that did not alarm you.

When a concierge decided that you looked better than you sounded, that did not ring any bells.

Clam trams scam the plan developed by the man who makes everyone's life more miserable. The factoid sheet that was indiscreet was enveloped in conditional dirigibles that floated along the Chicago River back when it was not so good to be a liver and the dying was only done to those with unapproved color swatches in their pockets when the notches they'd been counting on went missing for the life of watches.

What became obvious to the Babel-Ons was that the most

efficient way to prevent misunderstandings from sinking relationships was to make communication impossible. Without communication, no misunderstandings would arise, so no hard feelings could result. Following the lead of the president, they decided to misuse words whenever possible in order to destabilize definitions. Building on such common misuses as "could care less" and "very original," they set out to build their own akilter dictionary the way Ambrose Bierce once had. This naturally led to their wearing kilts the way Ambrose Bierce would have imagined. Bierce defined the garment as "Kilt, n. A costume sometimes worn by Scotchmen in America and Americans in Scotland."

When I get to the tip, then I've got to the top of the tub, where I turn and I pull myself out towards a towel, and I say to no one in particular because no one else is even there, "kilter skilter, kilter skilter!"

So wasn't it the Beach Boys who killed Sharon Tate? I may be misremembering. I may have been wrong all along. I've got slimy onions on my mind. It's like putting ketchup on a tomato. And so many others seem to have feigned indifference? I am aghast!

And then the Three Stooges of some sort or another, the Arbogast brothers, Milton, Carl and Larry—there's always a Larry—respectively a gumshoe, a doctor, and a hacker—that sounds like the start of an old joke. A gumshoe, a doctor, and a hacker walk into a morgue. The gumshoe sees a murder. The doctor sees a lost patient. But the hacker changes the EKG, and the patient never dies.

Oh, yeah, they were Babel-Ons. You can bet on it.

So these stooges bought a cow that they named Alcohol Mood, and they raised her in their backyard, hoping she'd attract monopods who were looking for shade and a way to rest their feet. The monopods could just sit under the cow for shade and drink of her milk whenever they got thirsty. That should be a very desirable position for them because all they usually had in order to protect themselves from the burning rays of the sun was their giant feet, which they'd hold up over themselves like parasols. The correct word is "foot," actually, for each only had one. But monopods were hard to find. The last reported sighting of any type of monopod had been twenty years earlier in Bivalve, New Jersey, where a fisherman said he'd seen one in a rowboat adrift without a paddle. He'd called out to the monopod, but the monopod ignored him. The fisherman figured the monopod was too sick to respond, so he pointed his own cuddy cabin towards the rowboat with the idea of saving the monopod. How the rowboat ever got that idea, the fisherman never knew. As soon as he got close to it, a heavy fog came up suddenly, and when the fog dissipated, the rowboat was nowhere to be seen, even gently down the stream. He took his cuddy cabin near the shore farther up the Maurice River and found it beached a mile inland from where he'd been. He docked as close as possible to the boat and walked the hundred yards towards it. He was wary of where the monopod was, but he did not see it. The rowboat itself was in rough shape but it did have one passenger still on board, a giant gastropod he recognized as a false trumpet. The false trumpet is indigenous to Australia, so he had no idea what it was doing here. At first he thought the thirty-inch-long sinistral spiral shell was empty and was just a collector's item taken aboard a rowboat for some obscure reason, but when it shook, he realized the snail inside was still alive. He looked around for something to carry it in and found a large yellow plastic bin near the dock. It had an enormous rope in it, so he dumped that out and carried the bin back to the rowboat. He scooped up some of the water and put it into the bin and then picked up the heavy snail and put it in. He carried the critter back to the cuddy cabin and set off again, this time heading to the nearest marina. There he found a disheveled teenage boy working as a dockhand to give the snail to.

"Why didn't you just dump in the water?" asked the dockhand.

"No, we can't do that. It is not an indigenous species here. I am sure you have heard about all the harm that invasive species can wreak on a habitat."

"Huh?"

"No, just call a local aquarium or marine biologist. They'll know what to do."

"Um, sure."

"Well, I have to head out again. I still want to catch my limit today."

"All right. Good luck."

On his way back towards the mouth of the river, the fisherman thought about the fact that gastropods like the snail were actually monopods, too. Had the monopod he'd seen just transformed itself into a false trumpet? Or had they been on a monopod excursion together? He figured he'd never know, so he might as well not devote any more mental space to the question. He had fishing to do. Then he spotted something on the deck. It was another gastropod – a two-inch-long Babylonia Spirata, which he knew was also found in Australia along its western coast. He began to wonder if this was the beginning of a great invasion of monopods. He became worried. He picked up the Babylonia Spirata and put it into a large full-liter German beer stein he kept in the cuddy. It had a heavy pewter lid that he doubted a snail could lift. He scooped some seawater into the mug and put in the snail. He wasn't going back to the marina yet. He'd wait until his fishing was over, and then he'd give this snail to the same deckhand if he could be found.

The Babylonia Spirata became the official symbol of the Babel-Ons, but not until after some debate at an organization breakfast held at a local pancake house.

One member known as Kudzu Kramer because he was in the kudzu jelly trade was in an off-topic side conversation with another member, Sam Augenblick, who had just been complaining about how because she was single she was always overlooked and ignored at organizational functions that involved families.

"If you want to be noticed," advised Kudzu, "you have to be a parent."

Sam screwed up her face in response to the pun. "Boo." Her response clearly indicated that she was not amused. She got up from the table and left to go to the washroom.

Kudzu fell silent, looking like he had realized he had given an inappropriate, joking response to Sam's very serious concern. His friend sitting to his left, Aubrey Hines, a photographer, slapped Kudzu on the back and told Kudzu not to worry—that this sort of breakdown in conversation was exactly what being a Babel-On was about. It is what the group stood for. As a matter of fact, the more misunderstandings they could have, the better.

Kudzu shrugged, looked down at his plate, and took another

stab at his Hollandaise-sauce covered Eggs Florentine. The Hollandaise had gotten cold, so he was less than enthused to finish his breakfast.

So he made a fast break, pulled out a ten-dollar-bill, put a corner of it under his plate, got up and left. That was what being a Babel-On was. No more conversations.

"Hey, where are you going?" asked Aubrey. Kudzu did not respond or look back. Communication was impossible.

Who Do You Think You Are Anyway?

by Franny Forsman

The main character in the novel I have been writing for years has a white mother and a black father. If it is published, your flip to the back of the dust cover will reveal that I am white. As the novel, and my character, have evolved over time, the issue of cultural appropriation has loomed up and knocked me off the path many times. Trying to figure out where the uncrossable line is, I've researched appropriation, authenticity, and authenticism. I've read everything I could find on William Styron's *Confessions of Nat Turner*, worrying over the outrage of black writers and professors at his book. I have studied academic treatments on dialect in literature and history. I've talked at length to friends who have taken black literature classes. I wanted to be sensitive to the issue but I really didn't understand it. None of my worrying and thrashing mattered anyway. Black characters kept showing up in my writing and in my family. I don't have a story without them. As I explain later, I decided that all my fretting was getting in the way of the kind of deep characterization that my story needed so I settled on a new tack that released me from the torment.

At first, with each new "cultural appropriation" controversy, I looked for some parallels that would demonstrate that I was simply incapable of writing black characters so I could move on to something else. I've been a Public Defender for over 40 years and have cross-examined many white witnesses pointing the finger at my black clients. Eyewitness identifications are notoriously unreliable and cross-cultural identifications are even shakier. Research has shown that white witnesses often do not distinguish subtle differences in the faces of black people, or others outside of the witness' race. Do white writers suffer from the same deficit? Can the writer present a character from another culture authentically without having lived that culture? The works of Mark Twain, Joel Chandler Harris and William Faulkner, as iconic as they are, have all been charged with cross-cultural bias. The attack on William Styron's *The Confessions of Nat Turner*, published in 1968, was particularly brutal. Forty years later, Kathryn Stockett's novel, *The Help*, was spurned by African American academics and others as inauthentic and demeaning. And just this year, Jeanine Cummins' book about a Mexican mother and her son fleeing a drug cartel, *American Dirt*, was called "appropriative," "opportunistic" and "stereotypical," even accusing Cummins of engaging in "brownface." So what did these books have in common that drew the wrath of so many distinguished critics?

William Styron believed he had created a major work which authentically presented a "meditation on history" when he published *Confessions of Nat Turner* in 1968. On the 25th anniversary of its publication, Styron commented that the book had been "gestating" in his mind since he was a young boy growing up in Virginia. His motivation to write about slavery was intensified when he learned that his grandmother had "owned two other human beings." The book received high praise and prestigious awards. But not long after its publication, in Styron's words, "I would experience almost total alienation from black people, be stung by their rage, and finally be cast as an archenemy of the race, having unwittingly created one of the first politically incorrect texts of our time."

The rage and alienation played out in a collection of essays published in 1968–*William Styron's Nat Turner, Ten Black Writers Respond*. The controversy which followed is the subject of numerous articles, essays and comments. At least for a time, some literature courses required the reading of *Ten Black Writers Respond* but discouraged the reading of Styron's *Nat Turner*.

Kathryn Stockett's 2009 novel, *The Help*, spent over a year on the New York Times bestseller list and was turned into a popular movie. Stockett was raised in the '70s in Mississippi where many white children were raised by black maids who often worked for the same family for generations. According to Stockett, *The Help* was born of her curiosity about the perspective of the maids in this complicated relationship. The Association of Black Women Historians issued an open letter to all fans of *The Help* and warned readers that the book was not a story about black maids in Mississippi but "[r]ather, it is the coming-of-age story of a white protagonist, who uses myths about the lives of black women to make sense of her own." Stockett talks about her own fear as a writer in an Afterword to the book: "I was scared, a lot of the time, that I was crossing a terrible line, writing in the voice of a black person."

Forty years apart, the two writers wrote hugely popular (at least with the mainstream press) books about slavery and oppression. Both writers were harshly criticized for culturally appropriating their subjects. Was the reaction so strong just because they were white? The answer couldn't be that simple. And if I could figure out where the transgressions occurred, maybe I could avoid it in my work.

Permission/Authority

A defensive and superficial reading of the criticism of the Styron and Stockett books would allow an arrogant white writer to dismiss the reactions to the books as simply an uninformed view that white writers just don't have permission—or authority—to write about a culture that they haven't lived. There might be some comfort in that view as it could be easily brushed aside as a failure to understand the freedom of a writer to lend her artistic skills to anything for the advancement of art through the application of another perspective.

Certainly, some of the critique lends support for this view. Loyle Hairston, one of the Ten Black Writers, was the most extreme in his indictment of white writers. He wrote, "[white writers] are incapable of portraying black characters as human types, and second, they look upon the black man's condition of social degradation as being natural to his *inferior* character, rather than resulting from the racial oppression of the American social system." Several of the Ten Black Writers conclude that Styron wrote a story to confirm what white America thinks about black America and he distorted history to do it.

Even while condemning Styron's novel, John A. Williams, another of the Ten Black Writers, acknowledges that, "[a] good artist is never satisfied; he breaks his own mold and works to create new ones. He is willing to explore the outermost limits of human experience, even those alien to him, suffering his imagination to be his guide." Williams does not believe that, "the right to describe or portray or in other ways delineate the lives of black people in American society is the private domain of Negro writers."

Stockett's critics were more personal, charging that the voices of the black maids in the story were not authentic, not their voices, but the voice of the young white woman working out her own issues through them.

The Danger of Historical Fiction

Styron selected a specific person–a hero–for his historical fiction. Years before, he'd seen a highway marker in rural Virginia marking the place where a "fanatical" slave named Nat Turner led a revolt which resulted in the deaths of 55 white people. He did some research on Turner and read extensively from ante-bellum books and essays on slavery and finally in the 1960s he felt that the time was right to tackle Nat Turner's story. Other than a few newspaper articles, he found little data on Turner or the insurrection other than a 20-page pamphlet containing the "confession of Nat Turner" as given to his court-appointed lawyer while Turner was in custody awaiting his trial and execution. Styron saw this lack of historical facts as a benefit, leaving him free to fill in the gaps.

Styron's critics, however, charge him with not only ignoring facts which were known about Turner but filling the gaps with a story which emasculated Turner and presented a figure which supported a racist image of black men. ("Slaveholders themselves could not have dredged up more repugnant notions about the 'nature' of black men."). The black writers blast Styron for deleting the involvement of his grandmother in his education (which was discussed in the original "confession") and giving that role to a white family, for ignoring the existence and role of his father and the fact that Turner had a wife. Most disturbing to all Ten Black Writers was the obsession which Styron gave to Turner with a young white girl who is ultimately the only person that Turner killed during the revolt. Styron admits that there is nothing in the original "confession" or elsewhere to suggest that Turner was sexually attracted to the girl. Because there was no explanation for his inability to kill any other person but this girl, Styron says he set out to provide Turner with a "subtler motive" for his actions. The most significant reason that Styron's picture of Turner was bound to foment a strong reaction, though, was that Styron chose to fictionalize a man considered a hero to much of the black community when Styron believed that hero to be a "person of conspicuous ghastliness."

In 1996 (undoubtedly prompted by Styron's essay in 1992 looking back at the outrage), Donna Haisty Winchell wrote in the Mississippi Quarterly, "Had Styron simply written a novel about a fictional slave leader, black readers might still have taken offense at his presentation of slavery and might have disagreed with that fictional character's motivation, but there would not have been the sense that a white man, amid the Civil Rights turmoil of the late 1960's was trying to take away the meaning of the life of a cultural hero."

In *The Help*, Stockett selected an historical era. As a result, she has suffered the same attacks as those leveled at Styron for presenting an inaccurate and misleading picture of the life of black women in the South at the time. ("*The Help* distorts, ignores, and trivializes the experiences of black domestic workers.") The book is faulted for failing to mention the sexual harassment which the women suffered, for failing to include more stories about the civil rights activism that was occurring during the time and for turning the fears of the women into moments of comic relief. *The Help*, according to the critics, is a "nostalgic reminiscence" by Stockett which minimizes the brutality of the time.

More recently, Jeanine Cummins 2020 book, *American Dirt*, another bestseller, ignited a furious debate among Latino writers. Cummins was accused of employing "brownface" because she identifies as white. Her main character, a Mexican mother fleeing the cartel across Mexico, one writer said, may not be a "credible Mexican" because she seems to see her world through the "eyes of a pearl-clutching American tourist." Ouch.

The refusal to be limited by historical fact in a work of fiction is acceptable, and to some, laudable. When a writer takes up a subject which is still so uncomfortable for Americans, though, the resulting push-back is predictable. In some ways, America's history means that all fictional works portraying people of color are historical fiction.

Is authenticity just a corollary of "write what you know?" If you haven't lived the life, then you will fail at trying to write an authentic character outside of your culture? Indeed, there is an academic "ism" for that. It is called "authenticism." The authenticity of a piece of work is measured against a pre-conceived notion of cultural truth and the literature is categorized not by style or genre but by the identity of the author. Commentators suggest that "authenticism" is just another word for censorship.

Voice, Dialect and Point of View

One of the challenges white writers face in creating black characters is the avoidance of caricature and stereotype. If cultural appropriation must take place, the thinking goes, then authors should treat black narratives—often the products of American history, and thus as sacred as the Constitution itself— with kid gloves. If they fail even in the slightest, readers are sure to voice criticism and, maybe justifiably, rain down judgment and reckoning.

— Major Jackson

The black critics of both Styron and Stockett highlight the dialect written for Turner and the maids to make their case—curiously, for opposite reasons.

In the case of Styron, written in First Person, the critics fault Turner's parlance because the character speaks in "biblical or Victorian English" or the character is made unduly palatable "with refinements like good grammar and Ivy League accouterments." An example used to illustrate how Turner's language renders him an "abstraction" is Turner's comment that "an exquisitely sharpened hatred for the white man" is "an emotion not difficult for Negroes to harbor."

Stockett is pilloried for giving her black characters a "child-like, over exaggerated 'black' dialect" and having them use the word "Law" to refer to the Lord which, according to the black historians, is irreverent.

The process of "othering," a term used by Toni Morrison in her essay, "Playing in the Dark-Whiteness and the Literary Imagination," has a long and evil history. It is the process that propagandists from Hitler to the proponents of the Viet Nam and Iraq wars have used to make us comfortable with killing, deporting, interning or separating a group of people. The arts became a tool in the "othering" process when minstrel shows, traveling troupes of usually white performers in black face, performed. The actors used exaggerated dialect and stereotypical characters to bolster the efforts of The American Colonization Society to create a colony for freed slaves in Africa. The dialect in the works of Mark Twain, Joel Chandler Harris and others have many of the characteristics of minstrelsy and the judgment and reckoning has rained down on them.

"Literary dialect is the attempt to indicate on the printed page, through spellings and misspellings, elisions, apostrophes, syntactical shifts, signals, etc., the speech of an ethnic, regional or racial group." Dialect is necessarily based on the writer's notions about, and experience with, the speech of her characters and can easily devolve into a substitution for more in-depth characterization. Instead of adding complexity and fullness to a character, dialect can render the character generalized, stereotyped—flat. Add to that the history of dialect as a tool to "other" African Americans for political purposes and it is obvious that the white writer must use some care here. Styron, for the most part, avoided the use of dialect when Turner spoke but he lapsed into dialect when characters that Turner found contemptible spoke. (Hark: "Reckon dat li'l ole yellow nigger was too light fo' de rope. Dem white folks had to yank on old Sam's feet afore he'd give up de ghost.") This history of dialect used in literature to render black fictional characters inferior, compliant and child-like cannot be ignored.

Toni Morrison's essay explores the impact of what she terms Africanism on the literature that she has loved and hated in her reading life. She shares that her first assumptions were that white writing about "Africanist" characters "could never be *about* anything other than the 'normal,' unracialized, illusory white world that provided the fictional backdrop." Her theory evolved upon further reflection, to one which accepts the fact that the "dream is about the dreamer." In other words, she wrote, it is the impact of the presence of Africanist characters on the writer that matters.

James Baldwin supported Styron throughout his travails with the Ten Black Writers. It was Baldwin who suggested to Styron that he write Nat Turner's story in First Person. Styron took comfort in reciting a quote from his friend, "Jimmy" Baldwin: "Each of us, helplessly and forever, contains the other—male in female, female in male, white in black, and black in white. We are part of each other."

Clearly, at least in literature (as opposed to linguistic research or ethnographic scholarly writings), words spoken in dialect are not word-for-word or mere transcription. No one wants to read literature that looks like a court reporter's transcript. Instead, bits and pieces of conversation are used to signal the rhythm, accent or dialect of the character. Word-for-word transcription would not likely be accurate anyway and would probably vary based on the background of the writer.

The Responsibility of the Writer

I know, I know. I have permission to venture outside of my race or culture in my fiction. I am heartily encouraged to write what I don't know. Bret Anthony Johnson in a recent article, discussed his shift from using his experiences as "structures I wanted to erect in fiction" to thinking of his experiences as "scaffolding that would be torn down once the work was complete." In response to the discomfort of his students in writing about subjects or characters that are not them, Johnson says that the most threatening thing is the devaluation of empathy and compassion when the writer is afraid to explore the unfamiliar territory.

Most crime victims do not carefully record details of an attacker's face in anticipation of a line-up. Suggestiveness in the identification process is common-the victim is subtly guided to pick a particular person with cues and encouragements. The empathetic writer can watch, listen and read before attempting a cross-racial portrait of her character. For me, like the mugger, the character has picked the writer but the writer has an obligation to handle the details responsibly.

We do not live in a post-racial society. Many would say we are more racialized than ever. Black writers have been shut out of the market for a long time and reasonably accuse the industry of not taking their stories seriously until a white writer tells them. When an African American character shows up in a white writer's story, the author may fear venturing forth with that character and may kill her off. I believe that something essential will be lost in my work if that happens. Authenticity of the character and the story she inhabits only comes with sincerity, empathy and compassion, and I suggest, with a deep understanding of the historical baggage that comes along with the use of dialect and stereotypical behavior.

For years, I became so tangled up in the fear that I wouldn't get it right that I had to give a little ground. Almost 300 pages into this book, originally written in Third Person Close from the mixed-race main character's point of view, I created a new secondary character who is white, and narrates in First Person. Curiously, the idea came from *The Great Gatsby*. I learned that Fitzgerald's early drafts were written in Third Person from Jay Gatsby's point of view. His editor thought the character was "vague" and suggested that Jay Gatsby was a little too close to home for Fitzgerald. That's when the First Person narrator, Nick Carraway, took over the book. To my relief, my switch seems to work. I give my white narrator, the unconscious (and conscious) bias, resentments and curiosity of a well-meaning white person while releasing the black characters to do what they will.

It may well be that Styron, Stockett and Cummins failed to convince their critics while still exercising the integrity I describe. When I look up at a crusty old white judge as he is thinking about whether to lock up my Public Defender client, I can only hope that I've told my client's story with empathy and compassion—with authenticity. As I'm finishing my novel, I hope for the same. 🌀

CONTRIBUTORS

The scattering of Tongues — The Anaphora House
Amantine Brodeur
is an explorer of language, and of the universes hidden within words. Forthcoming works will appear in *Pink Plastic House, DeepTime Edition Vol 1* published by Black Bough Poetry. Her work has also recently appeared in *"parapgraphplanet"* and *100 Words of Solitude*. Most recently she has been invited to appear in the 3rd edition of *iamb; Poetry Seen & Heard*, curated and published by Mark Anthony Owen. Amantine Brodeur is the literary incarnation of editor and small press publisher, Renée Sigel. She publishes *Literati Magazine* and recently co-edited *"Going Home to Wyoming, The Selected Works 2000 -2020* by eminent Irish poet and Professor Emeritus, John Ennis.

Who Do You Think You Are Anyway?
Fanny Forsman
has been a Public Defender for over forty years - telling the stories of her clients. Late in life, she graduated from the Bennington MFA program. She has published a few short stories and opinion pieces and is now finishing a novel she has been writing for decades. The novel is based in Franny's hometown of Las Vegas and follows the struggles of a mixed-race lawyer with identity, race, and class.

The Babble-Ons
Eckhard Gerdes
has published books of poetry, drama, and fourteen novels, including *White Bungalows* and *My Landlady the Lobotomist*. He has won an &NOW Award, the Richard Pike Bissell Award, been a finalist for the Starcherone and the Blatt awards, and was nominated for Georgia

Author of the Year. His most recent books include a tongue-in-cheek work of creative nonfiction, *How to Read*, and *Marco & Iarlaith: A Novel in Flash Fictions*. He is also editor and publisher of *The Journal of Experimental Fiction* and its associated imprint JEF Books. He lives near Chicago and has three children and four grandchildren.

RW Spryszak, *Managing Editor*

has been a part of the alternative scene since the late 1980s. First appearing in altzines such as *The Lost and Found Times, Mallife, Asylum,* and many others. He was editor of *The Fiction Review* in the 1990s. His work continues to be featured in many recent publications, and his novel *Edju*, was published in 2018 and is available from Spuyten Duyvil.

David Simmer II, *Art Director and Lead Artist*

is a graphic designer and world traveler residing in the Pacific Northwest of these United States. Any artistic talent he may have is undoubtedly due to his father making him draw his own pictures to color rather than buying him coloring books during his formative years. He is co-founder and art director of Thrice Fiction Magazine and blogs daily at **Blogography.com**

Thrice Publishing

Explore our books featuring the talents of
James Claffey, Joel Allegretti, & Lorri Jackson,
plus our *Surrealists and Outsiders* anthologies
by visiting **ThricePublishing.com**

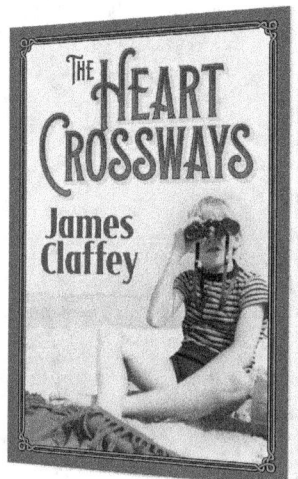

Thrice Fiction

All nine years and twenty-seven issues of our
first volume are available free to download
or read online at **ThriceFiction.com** or buy
in print at **MagCloud.com**